The Bl

M000304402

"In a perfect world, Bill Rowe's *The Black Storm at Elingale* would be required reading in every elementary school. It is about love: the love between brothers, the love between parents and their children, the love between neighbors, the love between soldiers, the love between people and horses. It is about power: the power of knowledge, the power of reading, the power of cooperation. It is about the elements of reading: letters making words, words making phrases, the key role of vocabulary to unlock the meaning of what one reads. It is about hope: each of us can do right despite our imperfections. And the surprising twists and turns of the plot keeps the reader engaged throughout."

—**MURIEL BERKELY**
FOUNDER AND FORMER PRESIDENT
THE BALTIMORE CURRICULUM PROJECT

"*The Black Storm at Elingale* is an engaging fantasy with a unique premise. Yes, this is a story of good and evil but in this tale the power being fought over is the power of reading and what happens when it is lost. A great story!"

—**RICHARD BOCK**
OWNER AND EXECUTIVE DIRECTOR
HUNTINGTON LEARNING CENTER®

"An engaging read with just the right amount of fantasy blended with well-crafted descriptions of people and places. *The Black Storm at Elingale* is a wonderful introduction to young adult fiction."

—**MARJORIE R. TANKERSLEY**
PRINCIPAL
HUGH MERCER ELEMENTARY SCHOOL
FREDERICKSBURG, VIRGINIA

THE BLACK STORM AT

Elingale

BILL ROWE

BLACK STORM AT ELINGALE

Editorial Production: Diane O'Connell, Write to Sell Your Book, LLC
Cover Design: Lisa Hainline
Layout: Steve Plummer/SPDesign
Production Management: Janet Spencer King, Book Development Group

Printed in the United States of American for Worldwide Distribution
ISBN: 978-0-9960489-0-3

"'Hope' is the thing with feathers—

That perches in the soul—

And sings the tunes without the words—

And never stops—at all—"

—EMILY DICKINSON

Dedicated to my mother, Elizabeth Grace

Author's Notes

I GREW UP IN a small house and a large family—eight children plus my parents. Peace and quiet was a scarce commodity. I enjoyed reading, but the chaos made it difficult to concentrate. One evening I was struggling through a book when my mother took notice. She told me I could go into her bedroom and close the door. This was a rare moment. My parent's bedroom was strictly off-limits when the door was closed. Once inside their bedroom, a wonderful silence engulfed me, and I felt a sense of privilege. I lay on their bed and opened my book. The muted noise fell away, and at that moment I was set free to ride a pirate ship pursuing hidden treasure or to float down the Mississippi River in search of adventure. Reading turned out to be like running away from home without the negative consequences.

Jump forward to present time and a new adventure begins. My wife, Sharman, a retired school principal, came home from a reunion with her former reading teacher, Maxine Blackman. Her school was located in a poor inner-city neighborhood, and the two of them had discussed the lack of reading materials in students' homes. Christmas was approaching, and they thought it would be wonderful if each child in the school was given his or her very own book as a Christmas present—something to read that was his or hers to keep. They decided that it was an excellent idea, but sadly there were no school funds to allow this to happen.

The spirit that drives a person to become a teacher never dies, so on her ride home that day, my wife seriously thought about how she could make this wish come true. At home, I listened to the story and agree that it was a great idea. We decided to call all our friends and family and ask them to donate to a book fund for the children.

We picked up the phone and started pleading. There were 300 children in the elementary school, and we needed to raise about $3,000. Because of the generosity of our family and friends, the fundraising task was easier than we had originally thought. With the money in hand, we had the daunting responsibility of choosing the *just-right* books. Buying three hundred identical books was out of the question, given that there were boys and girls of differing ages and various reading levels. So, with the aid of a local bookstore owner, we began our search. Our goal was to find books that the children would enjoy reading—hopefully, a few students would actually fall in love with reading and continue to do so through the rest of their lives.

One afternoon I was sitting on the bookstore floor with dozens of books surrounding me when I resolved to try and write a book myself. It seemed like a simple idea at the time, so the next day I began my authoring adventure. Each day that I wrote, I enjoyed the sensation of leaving my daily routine behind and entering the magic world of the story. I felt like Peter Pan flying out of the window to Neverland.

But it wasn't that simple; I also had villains to fight—not crocodiles and hooked-arm pirates, but saboteurs who were created by my lack of understanding of the writer's craft. I had no formal training in literature and made every mistake imaginable while writing this book. At times I thought I was crazy for thinking that I could master this art, but my wife and son encouraged me to continue.

The first few years, I used family and friends as my critics, but at some point I recognized the need for professional help if I wanted to publish my story. After doing some research I discovered Diane O'Connell, owner of Write To Sell Your Book. She enjoys working with first-time writers and said she would be happy to assist. Diane was the push I needed. Her comprehensive critique and revision plans helped me get to the finish line.

So, to anyone who has ever thought about writing their story but felt they were not good enough, I say don't let the technical stuff get in your way. This project took five years and four manuscript revisions to finish, but the journey was remarkable and the time spent was worth the effort.

Acknowledgements

With thanks:

To my wife, Sharman, advocate and first reader who unknowingly gave her unique name to the princess; to my son, Paul, whose writing skills and encouragement kept me on target; to my sister-in-law, Sue Rowe-Wenneson, whose copyediting skills and second read helped me along; to my friend and reader Sam Polakoff, who set an example by publishing his own book, *A Christmas Tale*, and kept reminding me to finish; to my niece and supporter, Ashley Meller, who critiqued my story; to Eric Seifter, whose scalding review tempered my resolve to get it right; and to Diane O'Connell and her staff for making this dream a reality.

An Invitation to my Readers

Come with me on a journey. It won't take long.

Leave your dull day behind and follow me to a land,

A land where the location is lost but the story remains,

Where the earth is still young and the moon and stars shine bright,

Where people live on a magical island lost in a sea of azure blue,

And the waves wash lazily over a beach of silvery sand.

If you care to know the story, come with me.

But remember...bring your imagination.

Prologue

*O*NCE AGAIN THE story surfaces," he told his brother.

"It doesn't seem possible. Tell me again; it's been so long."

"The legend says the bird brings courage, wisdom, and wealth. Its appearance has been known to change lives forever."

"But what does it look like?"

"Few have ever seen one, but they say it's the size of an eagle, though not a bird of prey. Its feathers are ruby red, and its beak is as white as ivory. The bird's most unique feature is a single, long white feather that trails from its tail like a wisp of smoke. Also, the legend claims that the bird can live for over a century; yet, it only sheds its feathers once in its lifetime. If you were lucky enough to find the white feather, good luck and fortune would follow."

"You said the bird's appearance has changed lives. What does that mean?"

"According to the tale, a beggar became a prince and shared his fortune. A coward fought a giant and emerged a hero. Another story claims that a dying man learned to heal himself and then prevented a plague from destroying his town."

"These stories sound impossible."

"Yes. But the legend says they're true."

"Does this magical bird have a name?"

"It has many different names in many languages. But we call it the Kookachoo Bird."

"Will we ever see this incredible bird in our lifetime?"

"Maybe."

<hr />

On a jagged cliff, high above the sea, a single tree clung to a rocky ledge. It seemed an impossible place for a tree to grow, but it had been there for over a hundred years. Atop the lonely tree's branches, the Kookachoo bird had made its home.

To the east, the black of night had faded, and the sun began to brush the sky with shades of gray and orange. The legendary bird rose out of its nest, hopped to the edge, and then leaped into the air. It fell several hundred feet before unfolding its wings and soaring upward.

As the red bird swept toward the sky, it accelerated its speed and then leveled off high above the azure-blue water. Its trailing white feather resembled a writing quill composing a poem across the sky. The bird continued to soar above the sea and then suddenly reversed its direction, whooshed over its nest, and banked once more, sailing back out to sea. Above the ocean, the Kookachoo Bird slowly dipped its wing and flew in a long, lazy circle, as if orienting itself to an imaginary compass. It then chose a southerly course and crossed over the rocky cliffs, rising still higher on the wind. As it sailed aloft, defying gravity, the Kookachoo watched the ever-changing land below.

In a flap of the wing, the high, rugged land gave way to timberland. Below, woodland creatures were scurrying about, but the majestic bird paid no attention. Off to the right, a river descended from the northwest, and the tall trees began to recede into gently rolling farmland. Villages began to appear more frequently, and little people were seen moving about while tending to their daily routines.

Still riding the invisible currents of warm air, the Kookachoo Bird sailed over a strand of silvery sand and beyond to the turquoise waters below. The nearly effortless flight had lasted less than an hour.

A curious distraction caught the bird's attention. Tilting to one side, it circled back and came to rest in a tree to observe the unfolding scene.

Chapter 1

STANDING AT THE water's edge, two brothers prepared for a routine day of fishing. Orange and gold light reflected off the calm sea while competing seagulls skimmed above the waves in search of food.

Thand, the older brother, brushed a lock of hair from his eye and examined the fishing net for damage while the younger, Eschon, made sure the weights were secure. When satisfied, Thand draped the mesh net over his left arm and waded several feet into the sea.

"Watch the master," he said lightheartedly, and with a quick twist of his waist and an extension of his arms, he cast the net into the sea.

"Good throw," said Eschon. "But mine will be better."

"Not likely," responded the sixteen-year-old.

The weights settled to the bottom, and Thand immediately pulled the handline.

"And anyway, we won't need a second throw; I've got tonight's dinner in the net."

Eschon inspected the trap and laughed. "I hope you planned on sea grass and broken shells for dinner, kin."

Eschon was two years younger than Thand, and the competition between the brothers was friendly.

"That was only practice. This one counts," said Thand.

Thand leaned back, ready to cast, and then stopped at the sound of a high-pitched scream. His eyes widened. A hundred yards offshore, a girl was wobbling atop a wooden sea chest, frantically waving her arms. The tide was turning, and the girl would be swept out beyond their reach if something wasn't done quickly.

Thand rushed into the water, and with a strong throw, he sent the net sailing toward the girl. She leaned out, grasping for the lifeline, but the awkward motion plunged her into the sea. The girl disappeared for a second, then emerged, coughing and spitting water as she blindly grabbed for the sea chest. Eschon had retrieved a cork-ended rope and was ready to throw it if it was required. It was, and the second toss went flying toward the girl, lost momentum, and then splashed down several feet short.

"Gotterslamit!" Eschon cried. "The wind is working against us."

"Don't pull the line back," the girl gasped. "I'll swim to it."

With great effort, the teenage girl pushed off the chest. Her strokes were weak; her mouth was scarcely above water. Then, just before she reached the floating cork, she soundlessly slipped below the surface.

Thand was already swimming toward the girl. As he closed in on the floating cork, he filled his lungs completely and dove downward. A small stream of bubbles led to the sinking girl. Her trailing hair was within his reach, so he wrapped his fingers around a handful of it and jerked upward. The jolt roused her, and then suddenly, she was kicking and grabbing at the top of her head. Thand knew he only had seconds before her lungs filled with water. He held tight and scissor-kicked his powerful legs back toward the light.

The girl broke the surface, coughing and gasping for air. She tried to push herself above the water, submerging Thand in the process. He pushed off the struggling girl and grabbed the nearby floating rope. Then, taking a deep breath, he dove back down, knowing she wouldn't follow.

Thand came up from beneath, hooked the line under the girl's arms and around her chest, and then resurfaced behind her. He put one hand on her back and lifted her chin with his forearm.

"Try to stay calm," Thand said, panting for air. "Hold on to the rope and lay your head back. The salt water will make floating easier."

Still confused and disoriented, she coughed out, "Who are you? Where am I?"

"You're safe now. I'll help you to the beach."

She closed her eyes, wiped the water from her face, and nodded.

The tension in Thand's body had just begun to ease when he heard his brother scream a warning.

"Get the sea chest! The sea chest—look, it's floating away!"

Thand inhaled sharply as he swung to his right. He didn't have enough strength to tow the girl all the way back to shore. Without the buoyant sea chest, only one of them would return to shore alive.

"You'll have to tread water," he said, removing the rope from around her chest.

Grabbing his shoulders to prevent him from leaving, she cried, "But I don't think I can. Please don't leave me."

He pushed her away. "There's no other choice."

Thrusting his open palms into the water, he stroked toward the retreating container. He was closing the distance when a painful cramp shot through his leg and stopped his forward motion.

He clenched his jaw, trying to block the pain, and continued to swim without using his legs. But the distance to the chest was growing longer. He rested for a second to reflect. *You're an Elwin,* he thought. *Use your fortitude to isolate the pain.* At that moment a euphoric sensation overcame him and the pain melted away. He kicked hard, and with a few more powerful strokes, his hand touched the sea chest. He wanted to take a deep breath and release the tension in his body, but behind him the sounds of a struggle commanded him to tie off the rope and return at once.

The girl was clawing frantically at the water in an effort to stay afloat. Thand raced to her side and locked his arm around her. Then, in a calming voice, he whispered, "I have you. You'll be okay."

All of her energy was spent, and she yielded to his touch immediately. Thand side-paddled to the chest and placed the girl's hand on the leather straps. He looked back to the beach and realized how lucky they were to have Eschon anchoring them to shore.

Eschon pulled steadily until they were in shallow water. Thand stood and waded over to the girl. She stared at him blankly, and when he reached for her hand, she wouldn't let go. He positioned his arms beneath her, cradled her against his chest, and then stood. With the girl in his arms, both of them breathing like these were their last breaths, he stumbled through the surf. Thand dropped to his knees and gently placed her on the warm sand. Several wordless minutes passed, and then a wave broke high, washing over them. Startled, she sat up and Thand followed. He asked if she was okay, but the girl just looked at him with a glassy stare. She turned back to the sea, wrapped her arms around her knees, and watched intently, as if expecting a ship to sail over the horizon.

Several minutes passed with only the gentle sound of waves lapping on the beach. The silence was killing Eschon, so to lighten the moment, he walked toward his brother and called out, "First time we ever caught a mermaid. Right, kin?"

"Funny," Thand said sarcastically, but the remark broke the silence.

Slowly, a smile formed on the girl's face as she realized what had been said. She turned toward the brothers, her frown gone. "I'm sure you would've preferred a mermaid."

The young girl struggled to her feet and addressed them properly. "I'm embarrassed by my behavior. I usually don't go to pieces like this."

She moved closer to Thand and placed her hand across her heart. "Thank you. I hate to think what might have happened if you hadn't come to my rescue. My name is Sharman, Princess of Adrianna Island."

She was taller than either of the boys but appeared to be close in age. There was a cut on her swollen lip and a purple bruise under her chin. A small scar across the bridge of her slightly upturned nose seemed to be the only other flaw on her face.

"My name is Thand and this is my brother Eschon. He thinks he's funny. Just ignore him."

She looked at Eschon and smiled. "Funny is good. But maybe I am in the land of mermaids, because compared to my home you two look out of the ordinary."

Eschon's posture stiffened. "Are you saying we're odd? We are Elwins, and we're proud to look different from humans."

She cringed, regretting her words immediately. "I'm sorry. I didn't mean to insult you. It's just that your ears are pointed and your hair is so thick and shiny. Your silver-blue eyes seem to glow with mystery. Actually, I think you're both cute and . . ."

The princess turned bright red and covered her face. Then, peeking out from behind her hands, "And I've said too much."

"It's all right," Eschon said, still a little irritated. "But you're the one who looks different around here. Red hair, green eyes—"

Thand interrupted his brother before he said too much. "Elwins are a mix of several races. Our ears are our most distinguishing feature."

Princess Sharman seemed to be off to a bad start. "I was so wrong to say that. You needn't explain. It's just that I'm so confused."

She rubbed the side of her neck while looking down at herself, and then she groaned. The princess wiggled and tugged on her dress, hoping to improve her appearance. Next, she dropped her head forward and combed her fingers through her long, auburn hair. She tilted to the right and pushed some hair behind her left ear, then looked up and caught Thand watching her. She gave him a self-conscious smile.

Thand cleared his throat, and then he removed a strand of algae that clung to her cheek. Her thin, oval face and muted green eyes were branded into his memory.

The princess was still not satisfied with her hair, but knowing it wouldn't improve, she reached for the bottom of her ruined blue dress and squeezed the water out.

"You'll have to forgive my appearance. I don't usually wear seaweed with this dress."

"On you, it looks good," Eschon said with a chuckle.

"It brings out the green in your eyes," Thand added.

The younger brother walked over to a nearby tree where a waterskin hung. Taking the container from the branch, Eschon said, "Drink this. It's fresh water."

The princess took the waterskin and nearly drained it. Cool water ran down her neck, and then, wiping her chin, she said, "I never knew water could taste so good. Thanks."

Thand noticed a silver chain with a gold key hanging around

her neck. The top of the key looked like the profile of an eagle with its wings spread wide. The shaft was round and carved to look like a long feather, while the end was shaped into two squares plus a triangle. *Maybe it's a charm and not a key,* he thought.

Princess Sharman handed the waterskin back and walked into the shade. Her sunbaked skin was burning. "I need to sit down. I'm still a little uneasy."

Observing her skin color, Thand picked up a container with a clear, oily liquid inside and handed it to her. "Here, wipe this on your skin. It will ease the pain."

After dipping a finger in the oil and lifting it to her nose, she asked, "What's this? It smells like coconut."

"I'm not sure," Thand shrugged. "An old woman in the village prepared it and told us to rub it on our skin when we're sunburned. It works on a lot of other pains too. Your lip and chin look like they could use a dose, but that cut on your leg will need to be bandaged."

"I guess I look pretty bad," she replied while smearing the oil on her blistered skin. "Well, at least I'll smell nice."

The girl sat on the log across from the boys, tucked her legs under, and smoothed her dress once more. A palm tree was just behind her, so she took advantage of it by leaning back and resting her head on the trunk. She took a deep breath and closed her eyes.

"This is the most comfort I've had in days."

Once again, silence descended on them. Then Thand motioned toward the sea chest and said, "I can't imagine how you got here. Will you tell us the story?"

Her posture slumped, and then, with a sigh, she said, "I'd rather not, but I suppose you earned the right to know."

Recognizing the pain in her voice, Thand insisted that she needn't tell her tale.

"Yes, I must. Otherwise, it will seem like a bad dream. And I owe it to my uncle to remember."

The princess scanned the horizon, as if looking for an imaginary object. A flicker of disappointment crossed her face, and then she began her story.

"I had finally convinced Father to let me go on a journey to another island, which was not an easy feat. My Uncle Warmund was the leader of a trade delegation and was to be my chaperone. I was very excited about traveling, and this would be my first time on a large ship. The first day at sea, I was welcomed by Captain Slater and escorted around the ship. Most of the sailors were friendly, but a few mumbled that it was bad luck to have a girl on the ship.

"The following day I was standing on the deck watching dolphins leap when all of a sudden an explosion shook the boat. I screamed and grabbed hold of my uncle. A pirate ship was bearing down on us and wanted the captain to lower his sails and prepare to be boarded. Uncle Warmund told me that if the pirates took control of the ship, they would kill anyone they considered useless—and the others would have it worse. I began to shake, but Uncle Warmund said that the captain had no intention of allowing Odyssey to be captured—he would defend his ship or die trying.

"The captain changed course and the ship pitched to one side. An extra sail was raised to add speed, and Odyssey began to veer away. However, the pirate ship was more agile and cut our lead in half. Soon, it was right alongside of us, and I could see a disgusting man with a scarred face hanging off a rope ladder. He pointed the barrel of his pistol right at me and said, 'She's mine.' Then another volley of cannon-shot flew into the rigging, and wood went flying. The main mast came crashing down, injuring several sailors. Another shot did more damage and set off a fire. I was terrified! What would happen if a pirate caught me? I ran for my cabin."

The princess paused and rubbed the back of her neck. Thand noticed a tremor in her hand. She took a deep breath, looked to the sea, and then continued.

"The pirates boarded Odyssey, and a terrible battle began. By then, I was hiding in the corner of our cabin with my hands covering my head. I could hear the sounds of clashing swords and screaming men. Smoke crept under the door, burning my eyes and leaving a harsh taste in my mouth. Cannon fire was replaced by gunshots, and screams changed into groans. Suddenly, the noise got louder as the cabin door opened and my bloodied uncle came running in with a soldier by his side. The man barricaded the door with a chair, and my uncle pointed toward the sea chest and said I would have to hide inside. I began to argue, but he told me to be silent."

Princess Sharman clutched at the gold key hanging around her neck and began rolling it between her thumb and index finger.

"He unlocked the trunk with this key and then hung it around my neck. I was warned to stay hidden inside until the fighting sound went away. I'll never forget the look of sadness on his face when he kissed me and said he would see me soon. I asked when but he didn't reply.

"The lid was closed and latched. I heard the glass window break and then I was tumbling. A hard jolt and a loud splash stunned me, but the trunk stayed afloat. I tried not to panic; but it was pitch-black inside the sea chest, and I had trouble breathing. I drifted for hours, which seemed like days, trapped in that cramped box, worrying about my uncle and the crew. My back and legs began to ache, and then I started to feel seasick. I couldn't stand another minute inside, so I pushed open the lid and breathed in the cool sea air."

Eschon interrupted, "But you said it was locked."

"All large chests in the palace have hidden latches on the inside. It rarely happens, but members of royalty have been kidnapped and carried away inside. My father ordered secret latches added to the interior walls, giving the captured person a chance to escape."

Eschon looked confused but said no more.

"I unlatched the lid and jumped into the water. It was so refreshing, but I needed to find the ship. At first, I didn't see anything but the rolling ocean. Then I turned back, and off in the distance, I saw smoke drifting across the horizon. The gray cloud led back to Odyssey."

Princess Sharman stopped, stared at her hands, and in a strained voice said, "How could such a wonderful adventure end this way?"

Thand didn't know what to say. He wished he could take away her sadness. But the princess straightened her back and continued.

"Splashing noises caught my attention. Schools of fish were jumping out of the water, and I thought they were playing. Then I noticed a dark shadow following behind. Sharks! I grabbed the top of the chest and struggled to climb out of the water. My wet hands slipped, and I hit my chin and split my lip—but that didn't matter because I was sure I was going to die. The shark lunged out of the water but only scraped my side."

Thand looked at the red line running down the princess's leg. "You're very lucky."

"I wish I was making this up, but I'm not."

The morning sun had shifted and was now shining directly on the princess's face. She raised her hand to block the light.

"Here, you can sit next to me. Make room, Eschon."

Both boys moved farther apart, and the princess squeezed in. Elbows were touching, but no one seemed to mind.

"Tell us how it ends," Eschon begged.

"Well, I'm not sure how it ends, but I'll tell you how I got this far."

Leaning forward, the princess wrapped her hands around her knees and then started again.

"The stars came out, and I guess I should have been thankful. But when I looked at the vastness of the sky, the blackness that surrounded me, I felt abandoned, forgotten, cut-off from the world. I screamed, 'I'm here,' but the words died on my lips. No one was there; not even an echo. I prayed for the sun to rise, to show me a ship or nearby land. At long last the endless darkness faded, but my sadness didn't. And again I wondered if I would ever see my family. Then I heard sounds behind me and turned. I shook my head and closed my eyes, but when you didn't disappear I started yelling and waving."

She stood and looked at Thand. "And thanks to your bravery, I'm sitting here, safe and in one piece."

Thand wanted to hug her and tell her everything would be all right and she was safe with them. But his voice faltered and all that came out was a weak, "It was nothing."

Eschon seemed to be forgotten, unappreciated, so he crossed his arms in front of his chest and said, "Well, that's nice, but what about the anchor guy? You know, the one who saved two people from drifting out to sea?"

Princess Sharman turned and gave him a hug. "The anchor is the most important part of the ship. I'd still be floating with the sharks if not for you."

Thand reached over and playfully clamped his arm around his brother's neck. "Come on, Anchor Guy, let's take Princess Sharman home."

Chapter 2

In less than a mile, the boys and their new friend reached the top of a hill. The teenagers set the sea chest down and stopped to catch their breath. Princess Sharman scanned the wide, gently rolling valley that flowed from west to east. Planted fields and low stone walls crisscrossed hills that were dotted with bleating sheep. To the right was a modest but well cared for village. At the western end of the valley, a large, stone manor house rested on the knoll of a hill. To the north, the hills grew steeper and grazing land was replaced by forest. Beyond the trees, standing in the hazy distance, a bald mountain rose above it all.

"This is it," Eschon said, extending his hand outward as if presenting a person. "Other people call it Elingale, but we call it home."

"It's lovely," responded Princess Sharman as they began to walk again. Birds chattered in the trees, and the perfume of early blossoms drifted on a light breeze. A stray cloud brushed across the sun as the three started down the hill.

"It's so charming and peaceful," she said as a butterfly landed on her cheek. The beautiful monarch seemed to kiss her hello before fluttering off.

Eschon thrust his chest out and took a deep breath; the valley had never looked so good. Thand looked away and rubbed his hand across the back of his neck, debating whether he should volunteer a more accurate picture, but days like this were rare— why spoil the moment?

The road branched into two lanes that ended just before the base of a steep hill. Neat houses, built from fieldstone and covered with thatched roofs, lined either side of the paths. Oak trees stood guard along the two lanes and provided relief from the hot noonday sun. A modest waterfall tumbled down the side of the steep hill into a shallow pool. The water ran back into a cave, but the villagers had built a stone wall around the pond and added flowering plants, transforming the area into a beautiful grotto. Behind the houses on the left, several acres of land were set aside for a community field. Corn, wheat, and barley grew in neat squares.

"Why is that field set away from the others?"

Eschon laughed bitterly. "It belongs to our village. The great Lord Creedy lets us grow our own grain."

"Who's Lord Creedy?"

"He's lord of the land. Most of us work for him—not that we have much choice. He pays us with a small amount of foodstuff like sugar and flour, mutton when we're lucky—scarcely enough to get by. Because of his so-called generosity, he gave us this field to grow additional food. Don't want to starve us. Right, kin? Dead people can't plow fields."

"Is Creedy his real name? It sounds made-up, like cruel and greedy."

"It's real," said Eschon. "If you meet him, you'll see that the name fits like bark to a tree."

"Let's not ruin the day," Thand said as he pushed his brother ahead. "It's time you meet our mother."

❖

A short, stone wall enclosed the boys' house, and a well-tended garden filled the air with the fragrant smell of flowers. To the right, a willow tree swayed with the breeze. Eschon ran into the house to prepare his mother for their surprise.

Thand led Princess Sharman into a modest-size room that served as a gathering place. In the center of the far wall was a fireplace used for cooking as well as heat. A ladder on the left gave access to a loft above the gathering room.

"Those two doors open to the bedrooms," Eschon said proudly.

Many of the village houses had only one bedroom, while others had none. Bedroom doors were a luxury his father had insisted on.

"How many bedrooms do you have?" Eschon continued.

"I live in a palace with too many rooms. It's cold and drafty at times with a countless number of people dashing about. Your house seems comfy and welcoming."

Thand brought his mother over to meet their guest. "Mother, this is Princess Sharman, from Adrianna Island. Her ship was set on fire, and she floated to our shore on a sea chest today."

"We saved her," Eschon added.

"Well, that's the best story you two ever told me," Grace said skeptically, then turned toward their guest.

The princess stood before Grace and gave a slight curtsy. "I'm pleased to meet you Miss Grace. It's true what they said. My ship was seized by pirates, and my uncle put me in this sea chest so I wouldn't be captured by the raiders."

Grace was a fit-looking, middle-aged woman. Her dark brown hair was pulled back and tied behind her head, revealing a few strands of gray. She wore a plain white blouse and a brown wool skirt with a green apron to protect her clothes.

The boys' mother reached out her hand to Princess Sharman and welcomed her. "I'm sorry for the disbelief. It's very rare that a stranger comes to our village. But I would like to hear your version. It really sounds terrifying."

Grace had piercing gray eyes that seemed to suggest that she didn't tolerate nonsense. However, the look didn't detract from her welcoming smile. She asked them to be seated while she retrieved the teapot hanging by the fireplace. As the tea was being poured, Thand began to tell a more detailed account of Princess Sharman's arrival and of her near-death experience.

When the narrative was finished, Grace leaned back and crossed her arms. "Well, that's quite a story. You're lucky to be alive."

"Thanks to your boys," the princess noted.

"They're good boys who had to grow up fast. When Boyne, that's their father, passed on, these two had to take over. Thand had to be a father and a brother to Esch. Most of the villagers respect Thand because of all the hardships he's overcome, and Eschon is following right behind. I don't do anything but cook and tend to the garden."

Eschon pinched the bridge of his nose and closed his eyes. Hearing his father's name brought up the memory of that awful day—the afternoon when the cart pulled up and two men carried his father into the house. He still remembered the conversation:

"What's wrong with Pop? Why is he asleep?"

"He's very sick. It would be better if you waited in the other room."

Over the next few days, many of the villagers had come to see his father. All of them had left the house with worried faces, and not a single person had looked him in the eye. The only thing either he or Thand knew for sure was that their father had gone to work that morning to clear a new field.

He remembered his parents' heated conversation: "As if Lord Creedy hasn't got enough money already!"

"I'll be careful, Grace. Don't worry."

"He knows what's living in that field. Isn't there some other place you can work today?"

"You know Creedy, Grace. Once he gives an order, no one's going to change it."

Little by little, the details had become clear to Eschon. Despite the known dangers, his father had been clearing a new field in an area where a deadly spider, named Mactabilis, was known to live.

Mactabilis! Mothers would use its name when they meant to frighten their children.

"If you two don't stop fighting, Mactabilis will come for you."

"You're as ugly as Mactabilis," was guaranteed to start a brawl.

Mactabilis wasn't an ordinary spider. It was the size of a large dog, with bristly, gray-and-tan hair that blended perfectly with the underbrush. The spider had multiple red eyes that looked everywhere at once. Eight legs and claw-like pincers made the spider fast and deadly. Mactabilis would hunt down prey, then rear up and spit sticky purple venom onto its victim. The acid-like poison would immobilize the prey and slowly liquefy the skin. This made the prize more digestible to Mactabilis and assured that the end of the victim's life would be slow and painful.

Eschon's father had languished in pain for three days before taking his last breath.

Suddenly, the sound of his mother's voice cut through Eschon's thoughts.

"Eschon, pay attention. You look like you're lost in a cave."

"I'm sorry. What were you saying?"

"I wasn't saying anything. Princess Sharman was speaking. Listen up."

"I was just explaining that I live on an island called Adrianna, but I don't have any idea how far or what direction home is from here."

"Do you have any brothers or sisters?" Thand asked.

"No...only me. I have lots of friends, but none my own age."

"What do you do for fun?"

"I ride horses. I'm a good jumper, but it took lots of practice before I could leap a stream without ending up in the water with my horse looking back."

Eschon chuckled. "Who did you play with?"

Her eyes brightened. "When I was young, I had a special room filled with dolls and I was their teacher—but unlike my tutor, I never scolded them. We would make up stories and then turn them into plays. I had a favorite doll named Evy, and we would climb trees and look into the town and talk about the fun we could have if my parents allowed us to go outside of the castle walls."

Her smile faded and her shoulders slumped as if an unpleasant thought had crossed her mind. Grace reached over and gently stroked her arm; the homesick look on her face was obvious.

"It's time to get you out of those wet clothes. You look more like a pauper than a princess. I'll get you one of my dresses; it may be a little short on you, but I don't think the boys will mind."

Blushing, the princess said, "Thank you. That's very kind, but I have clothes in my sea chest. I'll change into something dry."

Grace lifted a single eyebrow. "That sea chest has been in the water a long time. How could anything be dry?"

"Fortunately, the chest has been made watertight by lining the inside with oilskin. It's very effective."

Princess Sharman walked over to the chest and picked out a dry set of clothes and an embroidered bag. Grace showed her the sleeping room nearest to the fireplace and told her to change inside. The princess closed the door and removed her damp clothing. She neatly folded the garments into a pile, then brushed the sands from her arms and legs. Like any young girl, she fussed over each piece of clothing. Then, when her side-laced boots were tied, she stood.

The princess inspected herself in the reflecting glass, removed the last of the seaweed, and brushed out the tangles in her hair. Some curl was coming back as her hair dried, but she still seemed unsatisfied. After shuffling through her small bag, she removed a red ribbon, pulled her hair tight, and tied it into a ponytail. Then a quick tuck and pull and she emerged from the bedroom, wearing a white tunic, yellow skirt, and jeweled leather belt. She averted her eyes, unsure of the response she'd receive.

Eschon grabbed his brother's arm and whispered a little too loudly, "Wow." Thand brushed his brother's hand away and took a step toward the princess, but a stern look from his mother stopped him. Grace evaluated the girl, then gave her a bright smile.

"You look lovely. Now, I hope everyone is hungry. Eschon, take the bread from the hearth and bring it to the table, please."

When the meal had ended, Grace took Princess Sharman's hand. "I hope you have enough clothes because it looks like you won't be leaving the island anytime soon. The Elwins don't have any boats big enough to sail over the horizon. But don't fret. It's safe here. There is an unused loft up the ladder, and you're welcome to stay as long as you like."

Thand saw the color drain from princess's face. "Are you feeling all right?"

When all he got was a blank stare, he repeated the question.

"What did you say? Oh. No. Thank you. The food was wonderful. I'm very tired. If you'll excuse me, I would like to lie down."

Chapter 3

STIFLING THE URGE to cry, Princess Sharman slowly climbed the ladder to the loft. "You can't go home" is what she'd heard when Grace spoke. Her legs grew heavier with each step. *No ship to take me home, and no one knows my whereabouts. Where are my parents? Aren't they required to take care of me?*

Every part of her body ached as she crawled into bed. Her throat felt thick as she swallowed hard. Then the tears began to flow. She closed her eyes and the room started spinning. *Let it spin. I don't care. I'm tired of fighting.*

Princess Sharman tossed and turned while dreaming about her family. In the vision, she was in a dark, hot, and suffocating place. She heard the muffled voice of her mother calling her name over and over. The princess realized she was locked in her sea chest with no inside latch. She banged on the side and shouted to her mother, but no one seemed to hear. Her mother looked around the room, under the bed, and in the closet, but she could not find her. Then the princess heard her father say, "She must have run away."

"No. It's not like her to leave without telling us," her mother said. "She must have been injured and can't get home. I am very worried about her."

"I think she doesn't care for us any longer and will not return," her father said.

Then Princess Sharman heard her parents' footsteps fading away. Terrified of being left alone, she pounded more violently and began screaming, "I'm in here. Unlock the chest. I'm in here! Let me out! I *do* care for you." But no one answered.

At some point in the blackness of the dream, a tiny spot of light began to grow. Deep within a cave now, she sensed something was coming toward her. The spot grew larger as it advanced. Now upon her, the ghostly light revealed the specter of Uncle Warmund.

"A time of great change is upon us," he said in an unearthly voice. "The currents of fate have carried you to this land for a reason. Use the key. Its power will help."

"But how will I know what to do?"

The dream faded and the question went unanswered.

Princess Sharman arose late in the afternoon, clutching the key on her neck. No memory of the dream remained.

I must stop this self-pity, she thought. *I could still be drifting at sea, or worse. I should consider myself lucky to have found the Elwins. Not everyone would take in a stranger and offer them a place to live. I must find a way to repay their kindness.*

She sat up feeling lighter, as if a burden had been removed. Smoothing the wrinkles from her clothes, she walked to the ladder.

The princess descended from the loft to find Thand and Eschon resting alongside the ladder. The two boys jumped up like soldiers who had been found sleeping at their guard post. She laughed at their reaction. How could she feel sorry for herself when she had them to watch over her? She locked an arm around each boy, and they headed for the waterfall at the far end of the village.

This was the only day of the week that the Elwins were allowed to rest. As they strolled along the path toward the grotto, the princess was introduced to many villagers. They had inquisitive personalities and were unafraid of the stranger. Like Thand and Eschon, they were lean but fit and had the same riveting silver-blue eyes. Hair length was generally shoulder length in men and longer for the ladies, while color varied from sable black to dark brown. But not everyone had pointed ears. The young Elwins began life with round ears that grew more pointed with age. Eye color also seemed to be age-related, transitioning from blue to silver-blue and on to charcoal gray in the oldest ones.

Princess Sharman was eager to learn more about Elingale and asked as many questions as she answered. Through her conversations and observations, she discovered that both the men and the women were fit from hard manual labor. Many of the younger women wore their hair tied in a knot, creating a look that made their ears more prominent—a trait that seemed to attract the men.

The Elwins lived on an island named Lapis Lazuli. The name came from a blue stone that had once been mined there, but no one could remember when. The main occupation was farming, but fishing had become an important supplement. As the princess visited the local families, she found that they had all the basic essentials of life but were short on simple luxuries.

As soon as the trio returned to the house, they sat down at the kitchen table where Grace served them a portion of cold meat with warm bread. A wheel of hard cheese was already on the table, and hot tea was brewing. Princess Sharman thanked them for the tour, and some pleasantries where exchanged about the village. Then, shifting from casual conversation to a specific thought, the princess changed the subject.

"I haven't seen a single book or pen while visiting your friends today. How do you save your important information?"

Eschon looked confused. "Why would we save what we already know? Everything we need to be aware of is passed from the ancients to the village elders. They tell us stories from our past and everything else that's important."

"Yes, but events can be forgotten or changed over time," the princess argued. "Writing ensures that the information is passed down and not forgotten. Reading allows you to retrieve the information whenever you need it."

Grace, who was sitting nearby, understood what the princess was saying. She interrupted. "Lord Creedy forbids the existence of any type of school in the village."

Princess Sharman's eyebrows furrowed. "That's ridiculous! Why would he do that?"

"It's his way of controlling us. We only know what he wants us to know."

The princess jumped up. "Then let's change it. I can teach you how to read and write. It's not hard, and we could practice whenever you have some time free. I know how to make pens from feathers and ink from flowers. I'll show you how."

"Why?" Eschon shrugged. "It sounds like work—the one thing we don't need more of. Right, kin?"

The princess dropped her head, discouraged by his words. "I just thought it was something I could do for you. It would make your life better."

"How? My life seems okay," Eschon replied.

"I'm not saying your life isn't good. I'm saying that learning to read and write will improve your life, make it easier. You have nothing to lose and plenty to gain. Everything worth having requires work."

"I'm not afraid of hard work," Thand responded eagerly. "If you think I'm smart enough, I'd like to learn. I usually have some free time after setting the fishing nets."

"Fantastic! We'll start first thing tomorrow. Eschon, would you like to change your mind?"

Later that night, as they sat around the fireplace, the princess asked for additional information concerning Lord Creedy.

"What's he like?"

"Judging by the size of his pants, he's never skipped a meal in his life," replied Eschon with a laugh.

"He thinks everyone is working against him," Thand added. "And if you break any of his rules, you'll pay a painful price."

"It's a good thing he doesn't have a wife or child," Grace added.

"Why is he so mean?"

"Born that way," Eschon said with a shrug.

"People aren't born mean," said the princess.

"If you ever meet Lord Creedy, you'll change your mind. Right, kin? Tell her why we fish, and then she'll see," Eschon said.

Thand's hand tightened into a fist when he recalled the memory. "One afternoon, I was using a hoe to break up clods of dirt when I struck a rock and broke it. When Creedy found out, I was called to the Punishment Room. I was told that tools are expensive to replace—but Elwins aren't. He made me take off my shirt, then gave me ten lashes with his black cane."

The princess pushed back from the table. "That's *horrible*! What an awful thing to do. How could you be held responsible for a tool breaking on a rock?"

"It gets worse," Thand replied. "He told me to buy him a new tool if I wanted my food ration to continue, or I could use my hands to break up the dirt. When I told him that would be almost impossible, he told me that if I couldn't do the work then I was useless—and I could explain to my family why they would go hungry.

"I went back into the fields and did as I was told. I worked long after everyone else went home to his or her dinner. My fingers were bloody after the first day, and just touching the dirt was torture. Then my hand became infected, and soon it became impossible to work. I was burning up and had to sit in the surf to let the cool water wash over me."

"How can someone be that cruel?"

"The salt water must have had a healing effect, because within a few days the wound began to heal and the fever dropped. When one of the old villagers heard about Lord Creedy's punishment, he came to see me. He was an excellent fisherman and taught me his skills. One afternoon I realized that if I could catch enough fish, it would make up for the loss of our food. I asked Esch to come down when he could, and soon he was catching more fish than me. Within days we realized we could catch more fish than was needed. We shared the extra with the village and everyone had more to eat."

"So, you outsmarted Lord Creedy," the princess said with a smile.

After Princess Sharman climbed into bed that night, she began to craft an instruction plan.

I start by teaching them the alphabet, she thought. *Then I'll teach them how to sound the letters into familiar words. Once they know the letters and the sounds, they can write the words on paper. With their new knowledge, the Elwins should be able to write down their thoughts and begin keeping records.* She could hear her former tutor say, "Practice is the key."

The next day, lessons began. Princess Sharman was patient and repeated her instructions until the boys thoroughly understood. The speed of their progress surprised her. She wasn't sure how they were able to learn so swiftly, but the words "time of great change" and "enchanted key" nibbled at her memory.

That day's lesson was to write the entire alphabet in the sand. When Thand had finished making the letter *z,* he turned toward the princess and asked, "Why has Lord Creedy kept us from learning all this time?"

"The simple answer is, educated villagers are harder to control. You are dependent on Creedy for the basic needs, and this allows him to control you and use you for his own purpose. As your knowledge expands, you'll be become less dependent on Creedy. For example, after you learned to fish, you didn't need to work in Creedy's field. When you taught Eschon to fish, you educated him. If you wrote down your system, then anyone who could read could fish. As your reading skills improve, you'll be able to understand books that have already been written, and with this new knowledge, you can teach others on how to construct better tools, grow more food, and produce healing medicines. The knowledge you gain by reading will allow you to produce most of the basic items that you can only get from Lord Creedy. Then, as you learn to write, you can record your information and allow future generations to improve these skills."

"So, the more we learn, the less we need Creedy," said Thand.

"Yes." The princess clapped. *They understand.*

Back at the cottage that evening, Princess Sharman dragged out her sea chest and pulled out a tightly wrapped box that was lying in the bottom of the trunk. Inside the container were quill-pens, a few bottles of ink, and a large stack of paper. She had placed the items in the sea chest expecting to record her journey on the Odyssey.

"Look here," she said and held up two books bound in beautiful, handworked leather. One was reddish brown with the shape of an oak tree pressed into the leather. It was titled *Basic Science*. The other book, *Methods for Healing*, was tan with flowing, black script inscribed across the front. The princess had hoped to study these books while staying in Antilles.

"Inside these books are things that will make your life easier and information that will help cure sickness. But to unlock this knowledge, you must have the key."

Thand's eyes drifted to her neck. "No, it's not the one around my neck," said the princess. "It's here in my head—the ability to understand written words. Once you're able to read, the information locked in these pages will flow out and fill your heads with new ideas."

The boys looked quizzically at each other. Then Eschon decided to test her books.

"Is there a remedy for devil ants?"

"Let me look. What are devil ants?" she asked while flipping pages.

"They're red ants that make their nests in the soil. Normally, they don't bother anyone. But if you step on a mound, they'll swarm and bite you, leaving burning welts on your skin that will last for days. A large swarm can kill a small animal with their toxic stings."

The princess continued to turn the pages, and a minute later she said, "Here's something that seems similar to your devil ants. Do you grow a red pepper that is shaped like this?"

She held up the book to show them an illustration of the plant.

Thand bumped Eschon's shoulder. "Look! It's the piper-bush that grows near the edge of the woods."

"Let me look too," said Eschon, crowding his brother out. "Yes, but we thought they were poisonous."

"According to this book, you grind the piper into a powder, add it to some plant oil, and then wipe it on the bites. The pain and the welt should be gone in a day."

Eschon's eyes widened in amazement. "All of the bites we've suffered and the cure has been growing right outside our door. I wish we'd had that book sooner."

"It wouldn't be of any use to you," said the princess, patting the book with her palm. "You can't read."

"But if we learn . . ."

"Now do you understand how reading can help you?"

In the following days a strong friendship developed between the Elwins and Princess Sharman. She was caring and loving to all, but she seemed to have a special relationship with the children, who had begun calling her Dione-Du—the ancient name for second mother. Dull evenings were replaced with special games as writing and reading became the new pastime. Fill in the missing letter and spelling games were invented to make learning more fun. The princess created the Anecdote Award for the most amusing story each day. To be nominated, the tale had to be written on paper and read out loud. The winner was given a blank piece of paper and his own quill-pen to take home.

Treelore, the local healer, had borrowed Princess Sharman's medicine book and quickly learned how to make the piper-bush oil used for relieving insect bites. Before long, Treelore had a steady stream of customers. One morning, a young girl came to the healer with a blistering skin irritation on her arm. Treelore decided to experiment with the new oil and found that it also healed rashes. Inspired by her success, she began to read the medicine book daily and discovered other remedies for common problems. The new treatments were put in writing and turned into the first book ever written by an Elwin.

Treelore's creativity motivated Thand to examine a story on the subject of enriching the soil with decomposing leaves, and that led him to experiment with burying fish remains in the community field. His theory was written down with a footnote that the awful smell of decaying fish was also eliminated.

The benefits of reading and writing began to add up quickly.

Chapter 4

A PERSISTENT KNOCK WAS going unanswered. Annoyed, Lord Creedy slammed his glass on the table. "Where is my incompetent staff?"

He pushed his considerable weight out of the chair, marched to the door, and yanked it opened. A tall, dusty man, dressed in a fleece shirt and dark pants, stood at the door holding a leather pouch.

"What?" he barked.

"I've just ridden from your father's estate to deliver this letter from the overseer."

Creedy took the envelope and slammed the door in the man's face.

"As rude as his father," the agent mumbled as he walked to his horse. "Not a decent one in the bunch."

Lord Creedy returned to his chair. *What could this be?* he thought. *I haven't heard from my father in over five years.*

He looked at the plain cover: To Maxim Creedy. *Only my father would dare to address me by that name.*

Unconsciously, he ran his fingers around the outside of the envelope, contemplating the period of time when he had been known as Maxim. He began to recall that time long ago.

Kellen Creedy, Maxim's father, was a seller of cereal grains, such as corn and wheat. Kellen was successful before Maxim was born, but his father wasn't satisfied with just comfortable living—opulence was his goal. Living like a king wasn't likely, but he would make an effort. Large tracts of good farmland were needed if Kellen was going to increase his fortune. He secured a boat and went on a search that led him to the island of Lapis Lazuli. The southern end of the island had rich, fertile soil, suitable for growing crops, and the west side of the island had a natural harbor. The mountainous north was useless for his purposes, but that didn't concern him since the south had an adequate amount of good land.

On the island of Lapis Lazuli, land wasn't bought and sold— it was taken and held. Since that was already the elder Creedy's habit, it suited his strategy well. The island was mostly inhabited by a community of Elwins who were energetic but unsophisticated. *Easy to exploit,* thought Kellen.

Kellen proposed to the Elwins that he would teach them new farming methods using his advanced equipment. In exchange for their farming talents, he would provide all their food, plus construct a new village with stone houses that were considerably larger than the wood and mud huts they currently inhabited. "All your needs met—you can't go wrong," he pitched. The Elwin leaders thought more food and better homes was a fair exchange for something they were already doing, so they agreed.

Kellen Creedy may have believed himself to be a successful merchant, but Maxim Creedy thought of him as a detached and uncaring father. Maxim's mother died just after he was born, but Kellen didn't experience grief—instead, he was furious that his wife would leave him with young children. He refused the responsibility of being a father, so a nanny became Maxim's mother.

After some thought, Lord Creedy recalled that his father had

had two positive qualities. One, he'd understood the value of education, and two, he'd known how to use it as a tool for his own purpose. He'd told Maxim, "Think of education as a weapon: use it to your advantage, but keep it from your enemies." It was his father's best advice.

Lord Creedy dredged up the memory of his older brother, Wick, and their mutual dislike for each other.

Wick was a spoiled eight-year-old when his mother died. He was devastated, and since she died within a week of Maxim's birth, he thought it had to be his baby brother's fault. Wick's own opinion of himself was greatly exaggerated. He believed that he already knew the meaningful things in life and decided that studying was unimportant. But his poor judgment and inaccurate assessments would lead to several substantial losses for the Creedy Company. On one occasion, Wick failed to add a column of numbers correctly, which led to a large overpayment. Another time, Wick didn't comprehend the word *departure*, and a ship left their harbor before it was loaded, resulting in a huge loss when the grain rotted on the dock. Each time, he accused Maxim of negligence, but his father wasn't fooled. As a result of this and many other blunders, Wick was dismissed from the family business and expelled from the island.

With Wick out of the way, Maxim's ambition was to gain control of the family business. He knew Kellen wouldn't relinquish power on his own, so Maxim had to find a discreet means to make it happen. Some sailors had previously spoken of a wizard who lived in the north end of Lapis Lazuli. A few clever questions were asked, and soon he had all the information needed to make a call on a wizard named Baylock.

Baylock was aware of the Creedy wealth, and with a patron like Maxim, the wizard's wealth and reputation would grow. He was eager to help, and after some minor haggling, a price was agreed upon. The wizard prepared a magical powder to impair rational thinking. The potion was given to Maxim's father each day, and when Kellen was shown the number of errors he'd made, he agreed that a short period of rest was needed. Maxim sent him to recuperate in an isolated manor located near the center of the island. Servants were provided for his father's comfort, but their real assignment was to ensure that Kellen remained medicated and confined for life.

Kellen and Wick were gone forever, but Maxim still had one more name to remove—his own. A mandate was issued: Maxim is dead; Lord Creedy is born.

Creedy read the letter, stood up, and threw the paper into the fireplace. He called for his estate manager, who seemed surprised when he glimpsed Lord Creedy's face—the usual harsh look was replaced by a serene smile.

"I have an assignment for you," Lord Creedy said in a pleasant voice. "See to the burial of my father. No ceremony will be needed."

The following day Lord Creedy summoned the estate manager again. "Why hasn't the number four field been planted? It was supposed to be done two days past."

Looking down at his feet, the overseer coughed. "The Elwins have slowed down as of late. They spend too much time talking and too little time planting. I warned them yesterday, but they haven't made up for the loss yet."

"Please be more insistent and return with a full report tomorrow."

Did I say "please"? Lord Creedy thought. *I can't believe the loss of my father could affect me so badly.*

All of the next day, Lord Creedy's overseer worked alongside the Elwins, lending a hand while hoping to speed them along. He pretended to be friendly, asked simple questions, and listened carefully to the chatter. By the end of the day, the overseer had learned some surprising news and hoped to impress Lord Creedy. After changing into a clean shirt, he returned to the mansion in a hopeful mood.

Creedy was waiting in his office with his arms crossed and a scowl on his face. Immediately, the manager knew that his boss's attitude had returned to normal.

"Speak up, fool! What have you learned?"

"I've learned that an outsider from another island is living in Elingale. She was shipwrecked and two boys saved her from the sea. She has been spending her time teaching the Elwins how to read and write. The girl is supposedly some kind of princess, and she has been filling their heads with all sorts of new ideas."

Lord Creedy's chest tightened as he turned away. *So that's why they're not focused on work. Where did she come from? Why didn't I know about this sooner? Elwins learning to read—I forbid it!*

He turned around, a vein pulsing on his forehead. "No! This will not continue. You'll put a stop to this now! Double their workload and get that field planted, or I'll have you do it yourself. I want a daily report on the Elwins and their princess. This is my island and I won't tolerate interference."

Lord Creedy sent the servant away and then turned toward his study. A thought began to form in his mind. He stopped in front of the reflecting glass and stared. Caustic eyes and a pockmarked face glared back. Then, slowly, as his scheme became clear, Creedy's frown melted away and was replaced by a devious grin.

Chapter 5

*P*RINCESS SHARMAN AWAKENED at first light. She rolled over, trying to get comfortable again, but the straw mattress seemed lumpy. For the next hour she flipped front to back, back to front but never got quite comfortable enough to fall back to sleep. Finally, she sat up and massaged her cramped neck. She dressed and then climbed down the ladder to see Grace stirring a pot of porridge.

"Didn't sleep well last night? Sit down and eat—that should help. The boys have already left for the field."

"I'm not really hungry, but thank you."

"The circles under your eyes tell me you're worried."

"Something doesn't feel right. I can't explain it—maybe the heat. I must hurry. I'm already late for my students."

The vaporizing heat of the last two days was tamed by a light breeze and a thin film of gray clouds. The children's mothers took advantage of the cooler day by moving the classroom outdoors. When Princess Sharman arrived, the children's good-natured pushing and shoving ended, and a contest to sit in the front row began. A thirteen-year-old boy nicknamed Scribe, for his good penmanship, stood up and began passing out the pens he had made from eagle feathers. He had spent a week collecting and shaping the shafts and was hoping to impress the princess.

Princess Sharman's mood perked up the minute she saw the children.

"Good morning. Thank you, Scribe, for making these beautiful pens. I'm very impressed. And I'm so proud of all of your accomplishments that today we'll use the slate tablets and write the letters of the alphabet."

"We did that yesterday," complained a nine-year-old boy.

"Yes, and did we get all of them correct?" challenged the princess.

"Nooo...," the younger ones said in unison.

"I'll try to make it more exciting today. Write the first letter in each of these words: A Boy Came Down Each Friday."

The lesson had just begun when a large black carriage rumbled into the village. *LC* was scripted in gold-painted letters across the door. Occasionally, Lord Creedy's carriages were seen on the roads leading to the mansion—but never in the village.

The driver pulled on the reins and brought the horses to a stop. The trailing dust cloud overtook the coach and obscured it from sight. For a moment everyone just stared at the hidden carriage, and then the dust settled. An invisible sneeze burst from the interior, and then the whole coach groaned and sagged to one side as the door swung open. Mothers clutched their children as a brawny man with a hostile look stepped out. Light reflected off the head of the big man, who was called Shiny. A large mass of muscle was threatening to bust out of his soiled white shirt, and his dark pants were a boot-length too short. Shiny stood by the coach door scanning the crowd—hoping for trouble—a crooked smile on his face.

The lanky coach driver bounced from his seat and landed on the ground with a thump. His greasy, black hair was unkempt, and he wore a short, dark coat with brown pants that were several sizes too big. A piece of rope was knotted around his waist to keep the trousers from falling to his ankles. It looked like a stable boy had dressed him to be a coachman. The men's appearances seemed to suggest that proper clothing was in short supply at the Creedy Mansion.

The driver walked up to the princess, sneezed into his sleeve, and then said, "Our lord would like to meet with the teacher from Adrianna Island. It would be a great honor if you would ride with us to the mansion."

Princess Sharman looked at the coachman and swallowed hard. Her eyes narrowed in confusion. *How does he know me? Why would Lord Creedy want to talk to me?* She took a cautious step closer to the coach.

"No! No! Stop. Don't go with them. We'll never see you again," pleaded one of the mothers as she reached toward the princess.

The big man wasn't waiting for a decision; he pushed the mother back and then pulled a sack over Princess Sharman's head. The skinny one grabbed her legs. The princess began to struggle, pushing and kicking with all her strength.

"What are you doing? Stop. You can't do this."

They tossed her into the coach, and then the muscular one jumped inside while the other man climbed up to his bench. With a crack of the whip, the coach sped away, leaving the villagers screaming and weeping in a fog of dust.

Inside the coach, Princess Sharman continued to twist and kick. Creedy's man tied her wrists and ankles together and threatened to put a noose around her neck if she didn't stop struggling. Curled up on the carriage's dusty floor, the princess felt every bump in the road. The afternoon heat and the burlap hood made breathing more difficult; her mouth became dry with the taste of dirt, and her head started to ache. The big man kept his foot pressed on her back as the jolting ride continued.

Bumping along, the princess started to think ahead. *Where are they taking me? How will anyone find me? Are they going to harm me?* She was at the mercy of her captors and wanted to cry, but she willed herself not to. These men, whoever they were, would not see a tear from her eyes.

When the coach arrived at the mansion, Lord Creedy ordered the princess to be taken to the prison, located in the basement of his estate. With her ankles freed but the sack still over her head, she was forced down the stairs by the big man. She tripped and rolled down several stairs before hitting a wall. Crumpled at the foot of the stairs, she heard the sound of keys jangling, and something warm begin to trickle down her cheek. The jailer stood her up, pulled the burlap bag off of her head, and cut the rope bindings. Her hands began to tremble, and her breathing became jagged as if the air had been sucked out of the room. The color in her face drained, the room began to spin, and then a kick to her spine sent her flying into the gloom.

Shiny laughed. "Now you can teach the rats to read. Maybe teach them to sing too."

The big man looked down on her with a sadistic gleam in his eyes.

"Maybe I'll see you later," he sneered, then walked away whistling a mournful tune.

The rancid smell of death rose from the cold, rough floor. Cringing, the princess pushed herself into a sitting position and looked right, then left. *It's so dismal in here. What have I done*

to bring this about? I'm not a threat to anyone. Slowly, she stood up and scanned the room. The only source of light came from a small, barred window, too high to reach. Fear and anger mixed with doubt and despair. Soon her dammed-up tears began to shower the floor.

The princess slumped to the floor. Her palms and knees had been scraped red, and blood was drying on the back of her hand. She reached up to her throbbing head and touched a knot that was still growing. She also found a gash on her cheek that was still seeping blood. She tried to recall how each had happened, but there were too many sores to know which came from kicking and scratching and which came from falling.

The cell was frigid, and goose bumps began to rise on her skin. The odor of damp, decaying leaves mixed with a sour smell closer to the floor. One wall appeared darker than the other, so the princess reached out to examine it. Cautiously, she touched the wall and was repulsed by something cold and wet that felt like fur. She jumped back, thinking it was an animal. Her eyes adjusted to the dimness, and she reexamined the wall. The wet fur was not a beast—just dark-green mold growing on the rough stone.

Her arms grew heavy and her knees weak. She felt unbalanced and looked for something to sit on—a chair or bench—but there was nothing other than a pile of straw. She reached down and touched it—it was damp and smelly like everything else. Then the princess saw black fleas jumping and insects crawling through the straw. She recoiled and fell against the cold, rusty metal door, a final reminder that there was no hope for escape.

Crouched in the dank, creepy cell, the princess began to shiver. The clothes she wore were too thin. She wished for something warm and dry to wrap around her shoulders. A nice blazing fire and something to wash the bitter taste out of her mouth would be perfect.

Bitter tears formed as she fought back a sob. *Pirates, lost at sea, sharks, nearly drowned, and now I'm here, in this vile-smelling, bug-infested room. And no one knows where to find me. I'll never see home again.*

Thand, where was Thand? He would be her champion—break down the door and take her out of here, punish Creedy for his wickedness and then find a way to get her home.

Just then, something crawled across her foot. She looked down and saw a rat scurry into the corner. She screamed, but her cry went unanswered. Her sense of isolation increased, and by night-fall she gave up all expectation of ever seeing home again.

Chapter 6

A THUNDERING COACH RACED over the hill, threatening to flatten anyone in its way. Thand dove left while Eschon rolled right. Both disappeared in a cloud of dust.

Eschon hopped up shaking his fist. "You muttonhead! What's the hurry? Hey! That was Creedy's coach, kin. What's he doing in our village?"

"I don't know, but he doesn't deliver good news."

They took off running down the hill and were immediately surrounded by weeping mothers, crying babies, and villagers, all pointing toward the dust trail that was moving toward Creedy's mansion.

"What's happened? Is anyone hurt?"

Everyone started talking at the same time, but one mother seized Thand's hand, dropped to her knees, and pleaded. "You have to help her! Lord Creedy has kidnapped Princess Sharman. We'll never see her again unless you do something right away."

Eschon's face went white with rage. "That gutless coward can't come here and talk to the princess, so he kidnaps her."

Thand's stomach roiled. He understood Creedy better than most and knew that Princess Sharman wasn't taken to the mansion to have a conversation. But before he could think of a response, the crowd began throwing questions at him.

"How will we get her back?"

"Lord Creedy could take her anywhere."

"She may already be on one of his ships, heading out to sea."

Thand raised his hands to silence the crowd. "Somehow Creedy has learned that Princess Sharman is living here and teaching. He's frightened because we're learning to read and write, and he wants to put an end to it. He won't let go of her without a fight."

An emotional discussion followed as money, force, and logic were given as possible ways to make certain that the princess was returned. But then, the Elwins had no money or weapons, and there was no reasoning with Lord Creedy. After an hour of debate, no credible plan could be determined. The only thing they could agree upon was that Lord Creedy had the princess and they didn't.

A mother, holding a hungry child in her arms, suggested that it would be better to wait and see what Creedy planned next. Another mother agreed, and since no one had a better idea, the crowd dispersed.

Thand let out a long, low sigh as he walked away. "I've let everyone down, including Princess Sharman," he said. "They wanted answers and I had none. She needs help and we do nothing. I'm afraid he'll torture her, or worse."

A chill passed through Eschon. "You don't think he'll—"

Thand cut him off. He didn't want to hear the word.

"We're useless," Eschon mumbled while kicking the dirt. "It's no wonder he treats us this way."

Then, out of the corner of his eye, Eschon spotted a piece of shiny metal lying on the ground. He picked it up, then brushed it off.

"Look, kin, the gold key! It must have dropped during the struggle. Here, you take it."

Thand studied the key. Its design reminded him of the legendary Kookachoo bird. The key head was shaped to look like an eagle with its wings spread wide, while the key shaft resembled a long feather. Its weight suggested it was hollow or made from something other than pure gold.

Without warning, the shaft grew warm in Thand's hand. His pulse quickened as if energy was escaping the key. An invisible force seemed to flow across his palm and into his heart. The tension and stress of the day floated away on the breeze.

Seeing his brother's body relax and frown disappear, Eschon asked, "What's happening? Your frustration seems to have disappeared."

"I can't explain it, but suddenly I feel sure that we will get the princess back."

"How?"

"I just told you I can't explain it, but I feel there's been a shift in our luck, like a new season is beginning."

The sun was low in the western sky. Two days had passed since Princess Sharman's abduction, and still no news. Thand was out behind the house chopping firewood while his brother stacked it. Chips of wood, and curses too, were shooting across the yard. A rescue plan—which Thand had hoped for on the night they found the special key—hadn't emerged, and pleading with Lord Creedy's workers had only produced a shrug and a sideways shake of the head.

Thand threw a piece of wood across the yard in frustration. "I've hardly slept thinking about this. I have to help her! She's got to be in Creedy's mansion somewhere."

Eschon squeezed his brother's shoulder as a sign of support. "Kin, it's not your fault, and stop acting like you're the only one who cares."

Thand hefted the ax one more time, and then, using all of his pent-up bitterness, he buried the ax in a tree stump, as though it was Lord Creedy's head.

Crack! A gunshot rang out from the direction of the mansion.

Chapter 7

*L*ORD CREEDY WAS pacing the floor while slapping his black cane across the palm of his hand. The custom-made cane was designed to look like a hooded cobra standing on its tail, ready to strike. The silver head had ruby eyes and diamond fangs. The shaft was carved from black ivory.

I need to make her vanish, along with any proof that she ever stepped foot on my island, he thought. *Then, if someone turns up looking for her, I'll deny any knowledge of her. It will be my word against those worthless villagers. That's the easy part. The Elwins' ability to read and write is the bigger problem. Stopping them from reading isn't enough. The princess has planted a kernel of knowledge in their heads, and before long it will take root. It has to be pulled, like a weed, before it can grow and flourish.*

Lord Creedy chewed on the inside of his cheek while debating strategies. *A visit to my associate on the northwest coast of Lapis Lazuli might be wise. Wizard Baylock has proven his worth many times over the years.*

A devilish smile crossed Lord Creedy's face as he recalled an incident with a ship captain whose prices were rising as fast as his arrogance. By chance, Creedy discovered that the captain was charging him a higher shipping price than anyone else. No one was going to cheat him. He visited Baylock and purchased a unique potion designed to confuse the captain's sense of direction. North, east, south, and west—all would seem the same.

Several days after sharing a glass of wine with the greedy captain, Creedy was informed that an experienced captain had been lost at sea. The messenger left the room wondering why that kind of news would make anyone smile.

Baylock had never disappointed Creedy, but still, Lord Creedy wasn't ready to run to the wizard. Asking for help showed weakness, and Creedy's pride made asking the same as begging. Again, Lord Creedy picked up his cane and paced around the room, thoughtlessly tapping the floor like a blind man. Gradually, he concluded that complex problem-solving was the wizard's specialty, and with a sigh of resignation, he decided to seek Baylock's help.

An early morning directive had the stable manager hastily preparing the lord's fastest horse. He was throwing a saddle across the animal's back when Creedy's coach driver walked in.

"What are you doing?" he questioned. "We need a carriage."

"A carriage? I was told he wanted to ride north, not be driven."

The carriage driver smiled, and then, mocking Lord Creedy's stern voice, said, "Riding a horse along a dusty trail is absurd. A man of my stature must project power and wealth. I'm not riding a horse!"

Snickering, the stable manager bowed and said, "Of course my lord. You should flog me for my incompetence."

They both laughed, but the driver told him that they really did need to hurry. Again he used his Creedy voice: "My time is too important. I wait for no one."

With great speed, the two of them prepared Creedy's most expensive carriage—the black one, trimmed in gold, with white painted spokes, and polished brass lanterns.

Lord Creedy walked out of the front door wearing a gold silk surcoat and finely woven black trousers. A thick gold chain with a large sapphire dangled from his neck. Rarely did he dress this lavishly, but today he wanted to project his power and affluence.

He was carrying a walking stick that looked similar to the cobra-head cane, but instead of black ivory, this one was made of forged metal and sharpened to a deadly point. This was Creedy's signature piece when in public and was meant to be used as a weapon if needed.

A servant placed a step below the carriage and waited nervously. When Lord Creedy approached, the door was opened and he stepped up, settling into the luxury of the thick, padded seats. With a simple command, he began his journey to visit Baylock.

Creedy traveled comfortably along the flat, fertile land of the south, passing through the fields of laboring Elwins. Slowly, the rich land in the south gave way to rising hills and large expanses of tall trees. The smell of pine floated in the air, but even as Lord Creedy rode through the scenic countryside, his mind was focused on his wealth.

I could turn these trees into a great deal of money by building a lumber mill, he thought. *Maybe use the water from the Velox River to power the saws. I'd need a new road to transport the logs to my seaport, but that only requires cheap labor—and I have had plenty of that.*

Onward he rode toward Baylock's mansion. The timberland began to thin, and the ground became rocky as they rose toward the far end of the island where high cliffs held back the battering waves of the North Sea.

The coach arrived at the sorcerer's mansion two hours later. Lord Creedy stepped out and stretched. He tapped the serpent stick in his hand impulsively and observed the imposing stone house. It was big, but not as impressive as the Creedy Mansion. No columns or balcony, and the grounds were unsuitable for a lawn. A strong breeze carried the briny smell of the ocean and the thundering sound of waves crashing on the rocks far below. A shiver passed through Creedy as a reminder that the temperature was frequently colder in the higher altitudes of the north-end.

Lord Creedy walked to the front entrance, where he was greeted by a servant and led into a large, impressive chamber. The room was illuminated by shinning brass lamps that hung from the ceiling. There were no oil or candles powering these lamps— probably some wizard trick. As he tactfully scanned the room, he noted dark timber beams framing an arched ceiling. Expensive carpets from the Far East adorned the floor. A stone fireplace to his left was flanked by bookshelves, and from an unseen room, the pleasant smell of incense drifted in the air. The place had clearly improved since his last visit.

Lord Creedy observed Baylock sitting at a heavy oak desk reading a manual. The magician was large and powerful. His slick, dark hair was combed back with a part in the middle. The wizard had a short, neatly trimmed beard that ended in a tapered point. A curved, beaked nose separated ebony eyes with gold-flecked pupils that gave him a beast-like appearance. Baylock's stare could be unnerving. He seemed to look right through a person and into his soul. But Lord Creedy didn't flinch—he had no soul.

The wizard's gray wolfhound was lying near his feet, enjoying the warmth of the fire. The dog's ear lifted slightly as Baylock spoke in his deep voice.

"Look who has come to see us, Caedo. It's the devil's disciple, Lord Creedy."

Baylock looked up from his book, *The Nefarious Arts,* and addressed his visitor: "What do you want from me now, Creedy?"

"Such a warm greeting from someone who relies on me for so much," Lord Creedy said, patting the full moneybag at his side so that the coins clinked together.

"Not as dependent as you may think, Creedy. What's the latest evil deed you need me to perform?"

"I don't *need* you for anything, Baylock. But since you seem underemployed, I could use a simple little spell that will reverse the ability to read and write."

"So, the Elwins finally got wise and are learning to read. You can't have that, can you? It means you may have to stop treating them like they're worthless. Maybe they'll really smarten-up and get rid of you. Hah!"

Creedy pointed the business end of his cane at the wizard. "I don't need a lecture from you, Baylock. But since you asked, some princess from another island washed up on the beach and has been teaching the Elwins to read and write. I've dealt with her, and now I need you to erase what they have learned. I'm sure you can use your magic to create the perfect solution."

"Have a seat. This may take some time. By the way, do I detect fear in your voice?" Baylock taunted.

"I'm not *afraid* of those little people," Lord Creedy said, his voice rising an octave. "Just worried they would be harder to manage if they learn to read."

"Losing cheap labor—frightening." Baylock smirked as he left the room.

Soon after, a servant entered the room. He was carrying a

manual, but there seemed to be no book covering. String criss-crossed the pages, holding it together.

The servant set the pile of papers on a nearby table, straightened his lanky body, and then, in a monotone voice, said, "Wizard Baylock would like you to inspect this book while you wait."

"I don't take orders from Baylock."

"It's a request, sir—not an order. He says there are chapters missing from the book. Your input to the mystery would be helpful. I'll just leave it here."

Once the servant was gone, Lord Creedy untied the bundle and began to browse its contents. He raised an eyebrow; it appeared to be an account of an ornate quarterstaff. According to the story, the fighting staff had the power to alter the outcome of events in favor of the holder—an extremely powerful tool in the hands of the right person. He pulled out the desk chair and sat down. After an hour of close scrutiny, he sat back with a heavy sigh. There was no reference to the location of this staff. Was it lost, hidden, or protected by some powerful creature? And if it existed, where were the instructions to guide the holder in its use? Wielding such power would not be as simple as picking up the scepter and telling it what to do. Without these chapters the book was useless, a work of fiction.

Lord Creedy was retying the manual when Baylock entered the room.

"Isn't it intriguing? Despite the missing pages the thought of holding such power is worth further investigation," said Baylock.

"An incomplete fantasy story. I'm not interested."

"Right, I'll make sure you never see it again. But never mind that, I've consulted more than a few of my dusty tomes and have found an ancient spell. It was used by a king who wanted to silence an entire university for speaking out against his right to govern. It seems some students had been writing radical speeches, while others questioned his right to rule and researched his ancestry. But instead of sending in swords to silence the students, the monarch called on his grand wizard to find a solution. Within days, the spell-caster emerged and claimed to have invented a new spell. The enchantment is named Eliterate . It had the appropriate effect of terminating a person's ability to read and write."

"It sounds perfect."

"It's exactly what you've asked for. But there's a slight problem: the spell can be undone. The grand wizard was shrewd and wanted a way to reverse the spell if the ruler ever threatened him, so a secret phrase was hidden in the sorcery. I did some additional research and found the secret catchphrase, 'Reading is the key to knowledge.' If I understand the book properly, that phrase will unravel the spell."

"Unravel the spell? That's unacceptable! Under no circumstances do I want the Elwins to be able to read—*ever!*"

Baylock threw up his hands and spoke through a clenched jaw: "Will you listen for once and let me finish? These words to reverse the spell must be heard by everyone at the same time to be effective. The wizard knew that he could gather all of the students in the university courtyard and shout the secret words from the bell tower. There's no tower in Elingale, and no one knows the covert words."

"Was it ever reversed?"

Baylock cleared his throat. "I'm not certain."

"Not certain?" Lord Creedy said, flapping his hands. "At the price you charge, there's no way they should be able to break the spell."

"Finding another spell could take weeks, or months. If I have to make you a new spell, it could take years." Baylock clenched his jaw again. "Enchantments don't grow on trees, Creedy. It takes years of experimenting with words and potions. Sometimes a conjurer will die trying to perfect the spell. Meanwhile, the Elwins will become more resourceful each day. Take it or leave it. I have better things to do than argue with you."

Creedy turned away from Baylock. *More complications!* he thought. *It used to be so simple before that girl showed up. Baylock is right about time. Even if that princess never gives them another lesson, the Elwins can build on what they've already learned. I'm fed up with this problem. It must be solved today, not in a month or a year.*

"What are the chances of them unlocking the spell?" Creedy asked in a sharp tone.

"Almost zero. The Elwins know nothing of spells."

"All right, Baylock, but your spell had better do its job. I'm going to double their work. They'll be so tired when they go home that reading or writing will be the last thing they'll want to do."

"Don't worry, Creedy. I never fail, and I've already thought of a perfect way to deliver the magic. I'll put all the pieces in place and have the spell ready to cast in the next few days."

"You'll get paid when it's done. And I want a discounted price."

Chapter 8

*I*T WAS A pleasant morning in Elingale when Thand climbed in his wagon and set off for the grinding mill. The north-west road moved upward into the highland, leaving the fertile valley below. As he wound his way toward the mill, trees began to close in and cover the roadway. At one point the trail narrowed to single lane where the bridge crossed over the Ganzfeld River. This is where Thand always closed his eyes and trusted the horse.

The hour drive had been without incident, but as he approached the mill's waterwheel, threatening clouds began to dim the sun, turning a beautiful day menacing. A crack of thunder rolled across the sky, and he paused a moment to look over his shoulder toward home, where bright streaks of lightning reached for the ground. Thand shook the reins to speed up his horse.

He jumped down from his seat and walked to the rear of the wagon, where ten heavy sacks waited for him. Hefting the first bag over his right shoulder, he trudged toward the grinding mill.

Thand slowed down when he saw a friendly face. "Looks like Elingale is catching the worst of that storm. I hope they're okay," said Thand.

Before the man could respond, the foreman barked, "Get to

work! It doesn't concern us. So just do your job or I'll report you to Creedy."

Thand paid no attention to the remark and strode through the mill door. Inside, the groan of rolling stones and cracking grain made hearing difficult, while dust from the grinding process made breathing strenuous. Thand felt like he was caught in a dust storm; he dropped the sack at the designated spot and hurried outside for some fresh air. He wondered why the inside air was so thick today, coughed once, and then looked up to see that a second wagon was starting to unload. Thand knew the worker from previous trips to the mill and gave him a nod. The nervous man looked right and left, then, seeing that the foreman was not in sight, made a quick hand gesture to Thand.

"Over here, quickly," he whispered. "My missus works in the mansion kitchen, and she heard that Creedy has the girl you're looking for locked in a room below ground."

"Thanks. I know you shouldn't be seen talking to me, but I have one brief question. I heard a gunshot yesterday. Does she know anything about that?"

"I heard it too. But not to worry, a wolf got too close to the house. That's all."

Thand's shoulders slumped with relief. He nodded gratitude, walked to the wagon, and picked up another sack of grain.

Eschon placed his shovel on the ground, then stretched out in the shade of a tree with some friends. His stomach began to growl, but suppertime was several hours away. This was only a short break while they waited for the overseer to bring them cups of water. The rest-period left time for chatting, and like yesterday, the topic of discussion was the extra time that had been added to their workday. The field manager had told them it was "just until you're caught up," but no one believed it was short-term. A few boasted that they would pay no attention to the order and would leave the field at their normal time. Eschon chuckled; he knew it was just words. Creedy's penalties were too severe for them to ignore his orders.

Without warning, a worker jumped to his feet and pointed a trembling hand to the east. "Look! Out there!"

A wall of raging, black-fisted clouds was moving toward them at an alarming speed. The dark clouds grew larger, reshaping themselves and rising a thousand feet into the sky. Streaks of lightning forked out of the black mass, highlighting the clouds in deep purple; the air grew cold, and the wind blew a fine dust ahead of itself. The trees responded by shaking their leaves and giving notice that the workers might be in trouble.

Day turned into night as the reverberation of thunder grew louder and streaks of white-hot lightning became more frequent. Eschon felt the hair rise on his skin as a thunderbolt sliced into a nearby tree and split it in two. Half the tree looked as it always had; the other half fell to the ground, destroying a hay wagon that had been resting below. The wind and rain intensified, stinging the skin of anyone exposed, while visibility was cut to a few yards.

A father and son were running from the storm; they were crossing a dry creek bed when the intensity of rain suddenly turned the ditch into a surging river. "Flash flood!" someone shouted above the pandemonium. The father reached for his son's hand too late; the force of the water knocked the boy off his feet. He raced past his father, flailing his hands and shouting for help as he was swept around the bend. At the same moment another flash of lighting struck a large oak tree. It crashed down across the raging stream, forming a temporary dam. The young boy was swept into the obstruction, hit his head, and was knocked unconscious.

Eschon had trouble looking ahead as the biting rain struck his face. He put a hand in front of his eyes, hoping to improve his sight. Another flash of white light and an instant boom of thunder caused him to jump. That was close, he knew. And he looked to his right where the lightning had struck a tree. A small boy swept past him and slammed headlong into a massive tree branch. Eschon rushed over to the roaring torrent and tried to pull the boy out. The boy's father, Patwik, was frantic as he jumped in alongside. The current was like a vengeful man trying to pull both men down, but Eschon locked his arms around the tree limb, bracing himself against the river flow. Patwik locked one arm around Eschon, grabbed his unresponsive son by the back of his shirt, and pulled his son to higher ground. He looked down at his son's ashen-white face and limp body. He screamed like a wounded animal when he realized that the boy was not breathing.

Eschon came out of the water, trembling from exhaustion. He took one look at the unconscious boy and told the man to put the boy on the ground. "Push on his chest; get the water out. Hurry, you don't have much time."

Patwik sat the boy up and patted his back. *No,* Eschon thought, *that's wrong; you're not doing any good.* Without thought, he shoved the father aside.

"You should be pressing on his chest, not his back. Like this."

Eschon laid the boy flat on his back and put the full weight of his body into each compression. After the third push, the boy's father told him to stop, that he was hurting his son. Eschon ignored the plea and kept pumping the boy's chest. Patwik screamed, "Stop!" but just then, the boy shuddered and began coughing up water. The man gave a weak smile and picked his son off the wet ground. He looked down and saw that color was slowly returning to the boy's face. He rushed off toward the village, cradling his son like the first day he was born.

The tension in Eschon's body diminished—the boy could have died. He wiped the rain from his eyes and looked around to see if anyone else was in need.

Soon the rain began to subside and the wind calmed to a breeze. The gale seemed to depart as quickly as it had come, leaving behind a dazzling blue sky. The storm had lasted less than ten minutes, but the rain had turned the ground into a sea of mud that sucked at Eschon's shoes as he staggered across the field. Broken tree limbs were scattered about, and stalks of corn lay flattened on the ground. The frightened workers retreated from their makeshift shelters and raced for home.

The wicked storm may have bypassed the mill region, but the booming sounds of thunder and flashes of lightening hadn't. Thand was concerned about Elingale and eager to get back home. He shook the reins like a willow tree, but the horse wouldn't be hurried. They poked along at a frustrating pace, and soon the rhythmic sound of the horse's hooves striking the ground became hypnotic. Thand was lost in his thinking, speculating on the possibilities of a rescue, when the sound *ko-kook-a-choo* cut through his thoughts. He raised his head and caught sight of the Kookachoo Bird touching down in a nearby tree. He was stunned by the sight; blood rushed to his head. The beautiful red bird with the long white feather was real, not just a legend. The rhythm of time seemed to stop, and an urgency to communicate with the bird overwhelmed him. Inside of Thand's mind a voice-less conversation began.

It is said that your white feather brings good luck and fortune, thought Thand. *I hope you'll give me your feather to save my friend.*

You need not my feather to achieve your goal. Luck is a self-fulfilling prophecy if you are optimistic and plan well.

Open your mind, trust your instincts, and be prepared to take risks.

But how? The feather would be easier.

The Kookachoo Bird lifted its wings, then flew into the after-noon sky. Thand shouted, "Come back," but the words disap-peared with the bird. He lowered his head and thought about the brief encounter.

But I don't have the cleverness for planning and it's hard to be optimistic when you're discouraged. If I knew what to do, she would be free.

The wagon wheel splashed into a muddy hole and jolted him to his senses. Thand looked around and swallowed hard. Damage from the storm surrounded him. Small branches, ripped from their homes, scattered the area. A fallen tree, just ahead, blocked the road. Again he wondered if the last few minutes had been real. He pushed the encounter from his thoughts and maneuvered the last mile, dodging broken tree branches and deep puddles.

When he finally walked into his house, his mother was ner-vously chopping vegetables for a stew. Her eyes brightened when she saw him.

"I'm glad you're safe," she said and flopped in the chair with a sigh. "I was worried. Now, eat something and then meet your brother at the Samuel House."

"What's happened? Is everyone okay? The storm seems to have done a lot of damage around here."

"Just eat. A village meeting has been called, and you'll hear all about the storm there."

Thand hurried toward the Samuel House. He had felt detached all day and the deserted square added to the feeling. In the distance, he could hear the peaceful sound of water trickling into the grotto pool. The Samuel House was just to the right. It was an old cottage that had been left vacant when an elder Elwin had died and crossed into the afterworld. She had no living relatives and had told the villagers to use the house for a meeting place once she was gone. Since her passing, the house had been expanded and was now used as a classroom, but Thand remembered when it was used as a place to gather the children in the evening. A roaring fire would be built and the gray-haired Elwins would tell tales of a previous era. But tonight, the Samuel House was thrumming like a busy hive.

Eschon stood in front of the meetinghouse door, chewing the end of his finger.

"Where have you been? Were you hurt by the storm?"

"So this is where everyone is hiding," Thand said, as he looked past his brother.

"This isn't a social event, kin. A great deal has happened today."

Eschon quickly recounted a few details of the day before they stepped inside.

Clusters of people filled the room, with a storyteller in the center of each. It seemed that every narrator had a different version of today's events. Patwick had attracted the largest crowd by telling the story of his son's misfortune and rescue.

"Eschon, a true hero," were Patwik's last words when Scribe walked in and stopped the buzzing noise. Scribe had become the town historian, and he would record the evening events in a journal, just like Princess Sharman had taught. Scribe, like the others, had experienced the fierce wind and dark purple clouds filled with lightening; he had chosen to title his report "The Black Storm."

Treelore, the local healer, was carrying her self-made healing book, and Eschon had brought his stack of notes on weather. The details of the day's storm were going to be added to his weather log. A semicircle had formed around the three.

Scribe opened his notebook, prepared to document the day's event. He frowned and then raised a hand to rub his eyes. "Something must be wrong with my eyes. Everything seems messed up."

Treelore opened her book to see what remedies might help with vision ailments. Her posture stiffened and her voice became shrill. "These pages don't make any sense. They're just a cluster of pen scratches!"

Eschon looked down at his weather notes, then squeezed his eyes shut, believing he'd see something different when they opened. "This is the same—just a mishmash of lines! What's happening? Something's wrong." A murmur went through the crowd as other people started looking at the writings. They couldn't make sense of the pages either.

Thand walked to Eschon and looked over his shoulder. "What are you talking about? It's the weather notes from last week. Your scribble is a little sloppy, but this is perfectly readable."

"Not to me," Eschon said in an agitated voice. "This paper is just a jumble of markings that don't have any meaning. You see anyone disagreeing?"

Thand was still skeptical. "Are you telling me that none of you can read? That you have forgotten everything Princess Sharman taught you?"

Eschon asked some of the other villagers to try and read his notes, but none were able.

Thand looked around and saw the worry on everyone's face. They couldn't all be wrong.

"What's going on?" Treelore asked Thand.

"I'm not sure," Thand said, his mind racing through possibilities. "Has anything changed since yesterday? Something I don't know about?"

"Nothing—but the Black Storm may have something to do with it," Scribe guessed.

Eschon's eyes narrowed. "Did the storm strike the mill, kin?

"I heard thunder but the rain didn't reach the mill. I still don't understand why this storm has everyone upset. I can see it was pretty bad, but we've had worse."

Eschon looked stunned. "Pretty bad? It was the strongest storm I've ever seen. Do you know a boy almost drowned? The lightning and thunder were fearsome, and a strange dust blew ahead of the wind. It wasn't gritty like field dust but was more like ash from a fireplace, except sparkling. It covered everyone like whitewash and then the rain washed it away."

Scribe swept the room with his hand. "And now we can't read. That's out of the ordinary."

"So, not a single person can read but me. Is that what you're saying?"

"Maybe it's an evil spell," Treelore whispered.

Eschon looked at her. "Well, if it's evil it has to be Lord Creedy's work."

Treelore wrinkled her nose at the sound of Creedy's name. "Of course, who else could make this happen?"

"If Princess Sharman was here she'd know what to do," said a worried mother. "How will we ever get her back?"

The whole room turned to Thand. His chest tightened as they waited for an answer. His thoughts turned to the earlier encounter with the Kookachoo Bird. His instincts told him the villagers were willing to take a risk, but when he opened his mind to devise a strategy—nothing, just more questions.

I don't know what to do, he thought. *Where is she? How will we attack? What do we threaten him with? Should we surround his house?*

Sweat was forming on Thand's forehead. *What do I say? At least give them hope.*

"Creedy assumes we'll do nothing because that's what we've always done," Thand said. "If we pick the right moment, we can distract him long enough to get inside and release her. We have no weapons, but our numbers and bravery will surprise Creedy. Let's stand up and take action!"

Scribe gave Thand a wide smile. "Watch out, Creedy. It's our turn now."

The villagers cheered their eagerness to get Princess Sharman back home, but they were exhausted from the harrowing day. The villagers filed past Thand, nodding and shaking his hand like it was a reception line. When the room was finally emptied, Eschon put his arm around his little brother's shoulder.

"That was great. Now, how are we going to do it?" said Eschon.

"I don't know."

Chapter 9

*T*HAND AND ESCHON walked to their fishing spot without saying a word. A stiff, southwesterly breeze kicked up sand and whirled it across the beach. Unexpectedly, Thand stopped and threw his hands in the air.

"We can't continue this way. It's been five days since Princess Sharman was taken, and here we are, walking on the beach like it's a routine day. She's probably wasting away in a cold, dark room beneath Creedy's mansion and wondering why we haven't tried to help."

"Well, it's not like we forgot her or don't care, kin. We just can't figure out a way to rescue her. Maybe it's time we meet with Lord Creedy and explain everything, tell him it's not her fault, and then maybe he'll release her."

"Yeah, and maybe he'll give us all his gold too. He doesn't care about us or her. Something out of the blue will have to happen before there's any change."

Activity over Thand's shoulder caught Eschon's attention. He pointed to a boat being rowed to shore. They stepped back into the shadow of the trees and watched the men struggle against the waves as they attempted to land their boat. The boys debated whether to lend a hand, but the men obviously knew what they were doing.

Watching them secure the boat, Eschon remarked that the men were not from Lapis Lazuli and looked more like the men he had seen around the shipping harbor. The sailors were taller than the Elwins and had leathery skin, tanned dark from the sun. One had a short, dark beard and a brightly colored rag wrapped around his head. Another had a pink scar that ran from the corner of his mouth to his ear, like a one-sided grin. Four silver loops pierced the man's opposite ear. The third sailor was trim and carried a saber by his side with a royal-blue scarf wrapped around his waist. Having seen the boys earlier, the third sailor hurried toward them while the other sailors secured the boat. Thand studied the seamen, trying to determine if they posed a threat. The smell of sweat, salt, and tobacco filled the air as the third sailor approached.

The well-groomed sailor reached out his hand to shake and then introduced himself as Oden. He turned and pointed to a tall ship anchored offshore.

"Our ship, Trident Seas, has been searching many weeks for a missing girl. She's a princess, from Adrianna Island. Do you know of her?"

Thand tilted his head and looked past the man to his ship. *Is this a Creedy trick?*

"A princess, you say. Why would a princess come here? Tell me more."

"We're on a mission for the king of Adrianna Island. We're searching for his daughter, Princess Sharman."

Thand's eyes opened wide, but he remained cautious. "Maybe I've heard of her."

"We know Princess Sharman," Eschon called out, unable to stay silent. "She's been living here ever since we rescued her from the sea. Right, kin?"

Oden's shoulders relaxed as he let out a sigh of relief. "Thank goodness she's alive! Do you know where she is? We're here to take her back to her family."

"That could be a problem," Thand explained, rubbing the back of his neck. "Getting her back may be harder than you think."

Oden's brow furrowed and his posture stiffened. "What do you mean? Are you looking for trouble? I warn you, nothing will stop us from returning Princess Sharman to her home."

"Um, you don't understand," said Eschon. "A very dangerous and powerful person has taken her, and we don't know exactly how to get her back."

"If it's a confrontation you need, I have plenty more men on that ship," Oden said, pointing out to sea.

The tension in Thand's face vanished. "If you're here to help, we'll tell you all we know."

Assured that they were on the same side, Thand pointed to a bleached-out log and invited Oden to take a seat. The boys sat opposite but were too excited to stay seated long—they took turns jumping up and telling the mariners all that had happened since the day they'd found Princess Sharman floating on a sea chest.

"Does this master want money for the princess's safe return?" Oden inquired.

"No, Lord Creedy knows we don't have any, and besides, the last thing he needs is money."

Eschon jumped up. "We don't have any idea why she was taken. She's never done anything to Creedy. We didn't even think he knew she was here. Last night we tried to come up with a way to rescue the princess, but we couldn't."

"I have a suggestion," Oden said, leaning in toward the boys. "We'll join you and work together. I have resources on Trident Seas. We can beat this lord of yours and get the princess back at the same time."

Thand's pulse quickened as he looked at his brother. Eschon responded with a wide grin. Both seemed to have the same thought—here's help to defeat Creedy.

Oden asked for the layout of Lord Creedy's mansion and the number of people who worked in or around the main house.

"We can't give you exact information because we aren't allowed inside. But we'll tell you what we suspect," volunteered Thand.

Using a stick as a pen and the sand as a drawing board, Oden began to formulate a plan. Eschon insisted that everyone in the village should be involved.

Thand nodded agreement. "The princess is loved by everyone. It's important that the whole village be a part of the rescue."

Oden asked more questions, then told the boys he'd need a day or two to plan more thoroughly. Thand disagreed about the extra time for preparation and told him about the Black Storm.

"I've never heard of anything like this, but if the Black Storm did what you say, then Lord Creedy is afraid of Princess Sharman and won't keep her around long. It sounds like he has a powerful ally, so we'll only get one chance to make it work."

For the second night in a row, a meeting was held at the Samuel House. Oden stationed several of his men outside the meeting place to guard against infiltrators. If Creedy discovered the purpose of this meeting, he would execute the princess and destroy Elingale.

The Elwins were suspicious of the outsiders; however, the need for help was understood. In the beginning, the room was quiet, and most seemed reluctant to commit to any action. But the mood changed as Oden explained his plan. Before long, he had their rapt attention, and heads were nodding in agreement. When the meeting was over, the people left smiling and clasping hands with Oden and Thand. Their sense of purpose had returned.

At the end of the long, hot day in the field, the Elwins did not return to their homes as usual. Instead, they gathered near the grotto and waited for instructions. Anxiety was high as the villagers stood in line to have their torches lit. Some of the men, mostly young ones, bragged about their fearlessness. Some of the women, mostly mothers, questioned the wisdom of confronting the person who put food on their tables. Everyone realized the harsh punishment Lord Creedy was capable of inflicting. But this moment was about freeing Princess Sharman. So, drawing on each other for support, they gathered their homemade weapons and marched to Lord Creedy's estate.

Some carried pitchforks or scythes—their most powerful weapons—while others brought rotten vegetables and stones to throw at the mansion. When they were all gathered on the lawn, Scribe began the chant: "Bring us the princess. Release her now! We want the princess. We mean now."

Repeated over and over, the rhythmic sound kept the villagers focused and gave them a feeling of security.

Lord Creedy was sitting in his second-floor study, sipping on a nightly brandy, when the strange chant caught his attention. He pushed out of his chair, walked to a window, and pulled the curtain to one side. His eyebrows furrowed.

My, aren't the Elwins worked up tonight? he thought. *What's their problem? Maybe they miss their girl. I'll have to see what has them so troubled.*

Lord Creedy had no reason to fear the villagers, so he stepped through the door and onto the second-story balcony. The crowd hushed, surprised by Creedy's sudden appearance. He was rarely seen in public, and despite their dislike for the man, his king-like power awed them into silence. Some just stared back, waiting to hear Lord Creedy speak, while others began to doubt the wisdom of their defiance.

Stepping into the warm evening air, Creedy gazed at the crowd and was surprised by its size. The mood of the Elwins made him slightly nervous. The tools in their hands worried him.

He held a hand above his head to quiet the few who were still calling out and then gave a condescending speech in which he claimed to be concerned for the Elwins' well-being. He ended the windy speech by saying, "I have heard from the servants that you think I know the whereabouts of a lost princess. I can assure you that I have no knowledge of her, but—"

Boos and jeers exploded from the crowd; the villagers were fed up with Creedy's lies. Outrage had replaced hesitation, and someone tossed a cabbage, which landed with a splat on the white-washed brick, missing Creedy by only a few feet. He stepped back, surprised by their actions. His shoes would have to be cleaned.

"How dare you threaten me?" Creedy said angrily, but the noise of the crowd muffled his words. For some reason, the words of his departed father came to mind: "Don't underestimate the Elwins." With great difficulty, the lord swallowed his pride and held up a hand in an attempt to regain control. A moment later the noise softened. Creedy jutted his chin, put on a false smile, and then continued.

"To show you I have nothing to hide, I will help you organize a search party in the morning. I'll use my best trackers, and if there's a princess on this island, we will find her. Trust me."

"Trust him?" someone yelled above the jeering. "I'd trust him like a rotted bridge."

"He'll probably send us a three-legged dog that can't smell to do the searching," another added.

At this point, Creedy sent some men to guard the front door. The Elwins were more defiant than he had thought possible.

While Creedy and his minions were at the front of the house dealing with the villagers, Thand, Eschon, Oden, and his sailors slipped through the woods to the back of the estate. They ran to the stables where the hated landlord kept his horses. A raw-boned, grim-faced stable boy named Myke was scooping oats out of a sack, feeding the horses. Thand and Eschon's appearance startled him, and Myke grabbed a hayfork and jabbed at the air.

"Stay back!"

"No one is going to harm you, son," said Oden as he stepped in front of the brothers and held up his hands to show he wasn't a threat. "We just need to find out where the princess is being held."

Myke took a step back and aimed his weapon lower. "Why do you want to know?"

"We are here to free the princess and return her to her family," Oden explained in an even voice. "You don't need that pitchfork."

"Why should I help you?"

Oden walked slowly toward Myke, "If that was your sister in there, wouldn't you want someone to help her?"

The frightened boy realized that the men were not there to harm him and agreed, with some reluctance, to talk with them. He lowered the pitchfork and pushed a shock of copper-colored hair behind his ear.

"Yes, if it was my sister in there, I'd probably lead the way. Listen up, I don't like that no-good man and what he does to people any more than the Elwins, but I am forced to work here in order to help my family. Most of the people around here feel the same as me but are afraid to say it out loud. The Elwins know it too: if you don't work for Creedy, you don't eat, and if you cross him, the whole family will suffer."

"We understand," Oden sympathized. "Show us where Princess Sharman is being held, and you can go back to the stable. No one will know you helped us."

"She didn't do anything wrong that I know of," Myke said, trying to rationalize his decision. "She probably doesn't deserve to be locked up."

He sighed and tipped his head backward as if looking for an answer in the sky. After a moment he lowered his head and a look of acceptance crossed his face.

"Okay. I'll show you where she's being kept. Maybe it's time someone stood up to Creedy."

Myke led them out of the barn and across the yard. A huge oak tree provided cover as they crossed to the back of the mansion. When they reached a barred window on ground level, he pointed and said, "I think she's locked in the room down there."

"Thanks," said Oden. "Now, take me back to the stable and show me your two best horses. You're free to go after that."

Myke trudged toward the barn, doubting his decision. Oden reassured him that he'd made a good choice and urged the boy to walk faster.

"We need to hurry. I don't know how long the villagers can hold Creedy's attention."

Myke opened the stall doors and walked the two horses out. "These are Creedy's best horses. They're strong and fast."

"Thanks," Oden said. "Now go hide in the stable. Don't come out until you see us leave. If you say you fell asleep and didn't see anything, maybe Creedy will go easy on you. Thanks for being so brave."

Thand saw Oden coming across the yard with the horses. He tapped lightly on the window. No one had thought to ask if the cell was guarded.

A shaft of light from the setting sun filled Princess Sharman's cell. Another terrifying night of fighting off rats would soon begin. The room darkened as a shadow passed in front of the window. She heard a tapping sound, followed by a muted voice: "Stand back while we break the glass."

A sharp crack was heard. Instinctively, the princess lowered her head and raised her hands as splintering glass rained down. When she looked up again, a man was tying a rope around the iron bars of the window.

The sailors ran the line to a harness on the first horse. A snap of the reins signaled the horse to pull. The rope strained and the crossbars bent outward—but the rods held. They tried again with the same results. Oden became frustrated and called for the second horse to be added. Again, the reins were snapped. The stubborn bars held for a second longer and then jerked out of the wall. With the barrier out of the way, Thand and Eschon didn't waste any time—they dropped into the prison cell.

Recognizing the boys at once, Princess Sharman cried, "I knew you would come for me!"

She flung her arms around each boy and hugged them close while joyous tears streamed down her face.

"Hurry," Thand said. "There's no time for celebrating. We're going to tie the rope around your waist, and the men will pull you out."

She turned, pointed toward the door, and then whispered, "Guard."

Eschon moved to the door and stood with his back to the wall, knife in hand. Thand tied the line around the princess's waist and lifted her in the air as the sailors pulled on the rope. In an instant she stood in the fresh air. Wasting no time, the men untied the rope and tossed it back down to the boys. Thand took the knife from Eschon and told him to go first. Thand stood facing the door, white knuckles surrounding his weapon. A long moment passed but the dreaded sentry never appeared. Unknown to them, the guard had been summoned to the front of the mansion to help protect Lord Creedy.

The princess pushed the hair from her eyes and blinked twice. For a moment she was disoriented—the light seemed to be playing tricks on her. Then her hands flew to her chest as she gasped at the sight of Oden. The princess tried to speak, but her constricted throat only squeaked. Oden moved closer and held his arms out wide. She rushed toward him, then hugged him with what little strength she had. Stepping back but still holding on to his shoulders, she cried, "I can't believe you're here!"

"We've been searching the seas for months. I must admit we were worried, but we all knew you were tough. I never stopped believing we'd find you."

"Have you heard from Uncle Warmund?"

"No, not yet, but we have a second ship looking for him," Oden said, hoping he was telling the truth.

Eschon poked his head around the corner to see if they were still unnoticed while Thand watched the reunion with mixed feelings.

"We must hurry," Thand interrupted. "Our deception could fall apart at any moment."

Oden carefully lifted the gaunt princess onto the horse. Thand jumped up behind her. He placed one hand around her thin waist and the other on the reins. He leaned toward her ear, ignoring the sour smell of her clothing. "A great deal has happened since you were taken, but first we must get you away from here."

Eschon relaxed when the pair had faded into the darkening lane. He watched the sailors disappear into the trees, then stood alone, reflecting on the second part of their rescue plan.

Actually, we don't have a second part, he realized. *Princess Sharman may be safe, but what will happen in Elingale when Lord Creedy finds she's gone? Did we really think that he would act like this never happened and that life would return to normal? This will change everything.*

Swallowing hard, he rushed to the front of the mansion and slipped into the crowd. The hoot of a barn owl was heard twice, and the villagers knew that the plan had worked. Immediately, the Elwins' moods brightened—the princess was out of danger.

Treelore shouted to Creedy, "Keep your three-legged dog and blind tracker; we'll search on our own." A few more insults were called out, and then everyone turned and walked away. Lord Creedy looked confused but happy to see the Elwins withdraw.

Thand galloped down the lane, holding the princess tight. The sound of beating hooves made conversation impossible, but Thand was enjoying the intimacy. He wished the ride to the beach was longer, but it was more important that the princess be on the ship before Creedy realized he had been tricked.

They dismounted where the trees met the beach. Gentle waves and fragrant hibiscus flowers greeted them—a perfect setting for a quiet moment. Princess Sharman took advantage of the opportunity. She drew Thand's hands toward her face, then kissed each palm in the traditional expression of gratitude.

"Thank you so much. It seems that you've saved my life once more. Perhaps I need a champion to keep me safe."

Thand blushed. "Where do I sign up for the job?"

"Your first duty will be to teach me how to stay out of trouble," she said with a twinkle in her eyes.

"Maybe you could teach me how to *get* in trouble," Thand said with a frisky smile.

The crunch of running feet stopped their banter, and before the sailor could take notice, Princess Sharman dropped Thand's hands and stepped back. The panting man asked if she was all right.

"Just cuts, bruises, rat bites, and hunger," she responded. "But for now, fresh water would be nice."

The sailor found a flagon of fresh water in the longboat and brought it to her. Just as she began to drink, Oden appeared, breathing hard and running straight toward her.

"Hurry," Oden said, and he grabbed her hand while pulling her toward the sea. The container of water fell to the ground, but before she could protest, he hoisted her into the boat. Then, looking over his shoulder, he said, "I'm sorry, Thand, but we don't have time for a reunion. My orders are to get the princess back on the ship without delay. I hope to see you again. Thank everyone for their help."

As the sailors dug their oars into the surf, Princess Sharman turned and shouted, "Tomorrow. I promise."

Chapter 10

*T*HE RED-AND-GOLD HORIZON faded to hues of gray as the sailors rowed back to the ship. Princess Sharman was free from danger for the first time since her abduction, but her mood reflected annoyance. She was upset with Oden for treating Thand like he was trivial. No one on this boat seemed to realize that she wouldn't be alive if not for him. She intended to go straight to the captain's cabin after boarding. She would correct that false perception and then make her case for returning to Elingale in the morning.

When offered, she brushed off Oden's helping hand and climbed aboard. Across the deck she could see the captain walking toward the companionway. He was a heavy man with a hitch in his step that made him look lame, but anyone who mistook this for a weakness was a fool. The princess managed to catch up to him just before he shut the door to his cabin.

"Captain Boreas, I'd like a word with you."

"Come in, lass. I'm so glad to see ya," the captain said as he pulled a chair out for the princess. "We were worried about ya."

The princess sat opposite the captain, ready to confront him. A bushy, black moustache, flecked with gray, stood out against his nearly white beard. His head was shaved bald, so a design inked into the crown of his head was visible. The image was said to be Polaris, a star that helped sailors find north. There was probably an interesting story associated with the tattoo, but the princess wasn't interested.

She spoke about the courage of the Elwins, especially Thand and Eschon. Then, leaving the rescue story to someone else, she spoke about the kindness and generosity of the Elwins, the unpleasant conditions in which they worked, and their lack of education. She explained the necessity of returning to Elingale and the need to resume her teaching.

"I hear ya," the captain said. "But Lord Creedy will have to be dealt with before ya can safely set foot on the island. At this time, I don't have the resources or permission to confront him. Maybe ya can return sometime in the future, but right now I need to get ya home. No delays."

"Maybe it wouldn't be a good idea to return to teaching right now, but I still need to go back and talk to Thand and Eschon."

"Can't let ya."

The princess scrubbed her hands over her face and sighed. She thought for a moment, then raised her head. "You're the captain of the ship, and I know I must follow your orders. But wouldn't it be smart to have someone who can answer all the questions the king might have? If Thand and Eschon traveled back with us, they could tell my father exactly what has happened since I was rescued. They could explain my kidnapping and conflict with Lord Creedy better than I."

"Maybe."

"You need to understand that after all the Elwins have done for me, I just can't sail away like they'd never existed. They saved my life—twice. You've been at sea for several months now, and

I'm sure you have no specific date set for our return. One extra day wouldn't matter—not at this point."

Captain Boreas glanced around uneasily as he seemed to give the princess's appeal some thought.

"Ya make yar point, but safety is my main concern. Suppose Lord Creedy's men are waiting on the shore, just hoping ya show up?"

"The Elwins weren't worried about their safety when they pulled me out of that dungeon. I can't abandon them! I won't!"

"Ya've certainly grown stubborn since I last saw ya."

"I'm not trying to be defiant, but think how much easier your job will be if someone else could help explain this misadventure to King Treutlen. I'm still not sure how I got from the sea chest to the shore. And do you want to explain why you abandoned someone who saved the king's daughter?"

"Certainly not, but yar father would never forgive me if something happened to ya after having ya safely aboard the ship."

Princess Sharman leaned back and crossed her arms, her eyebrows furrowed and the pupils of her green eyes constricted. The captain wasn't used to such brazenness. His authority was absolute. He clenched his jaw and tried to stare the princess into submission. For several moments, the creak of the ship was the only sound heard.

Finally, the captain broke the icy silence.

"I know that look. It's the same stubborn one yar father uses when he can't be persuaded to change his mind. I'll probably be hung from the yardarm for doing this, but okay, I'll let ya return in the morning with Oden and a few guards. But ya better not disobey him. I'm going to give him specific orders not to let ya out of his sight. And I'm sailing with the tide tomorrow night. So ya'd better be back aboard or ya'll be swimming for home. Now go."

The princess jumped up with delight, ran to the captain, and wiped the grumpy look off of his face with an affectionate kiss on his bald head.

In the morning, Oden was ordered back to the island in search of the boys. The wind had been blowing most of the night, and white-capped waves crashed loudly against the ship. Looking over the side, Oden could see that launching the longboat would be more difficult than usual. Timing the release of the boat would be tricky considering the rising and falling of the waves. His sailors had been trained for this, but going over the side under these conditions was always dangerous. And the sea rarely forgave a mistake.

Princess Sharman looked over the rail at the whitecaps and almost changed her mind, but after last night's performance, she had no choice. She climbed aboard and pulled a canvas sheet over her head, hoping to conceal herself from any of Lord Creedy's lookouts. Protection from the elements was an added bonus the crew didn't have.

The adventurous men climbed in, and the boat was slowly lowered toward the sea. The waves continued to slam into the ship, drenching everyone with stinging salt water. The minute the longboat reached water, Oden released them from the ship. Now the real battle began as the boat rose six feet, then plunged. The next wave hit broadside and slammed them back into the hull. Again, a wave ran in and lifted the boat high, but Oden used this roller to his advantage and shoved off the bigger ship. They slid down the face of the wave and into the open sea.

While the sailors pulled on the oars, Oden surveyed the island. Thand and Eschon were on the beach, struggling to throw their net into the white-capped water, but the wind twisted their fishing gear and then threw it back into their faces.

Eschon was attempting to get his uncooperative brother to

help untangle the net when the longboat was spotted. Thand dropped everything and ran into the heavy surf.

"Is the princess with you?" Thand shouted above the sound of crashing waves.

"Stand to the side, boy!" Oden bellowed. "Do you want to be crushed? Let me get on land first."

The boat was lifted by an oncoming wave and slammed onto the beach. The crew jumped out and secured the boat before it backwashed into the sea. Thand was standing in the foamy water, scanning the boat for the princess. His shoulders slumped.

"I thought she'd be with you."

Oden shrugged his shoulder. "She had some hesitation—huge waves out there."

Thand looked down and turned away.

Princess Sharman struggled to find the edge of the covering. But Eschon saw the canvas move, and with a sweeping gesture, he pulled the sailcloth back.

"You're back so soon! I knew you couldn't stay away."

"I said I would return. I always keep a promise."

The sound of her voice brightened Thand's face. He reversed his course immediately and nearly tripped as he returned to the side of the boat. Then the princess reached for his hand and climbed over the side. They held on to each other a little longer than necessary.

"We can only stay a short time, so I'd like to go back to your house and discuss an idea. Your mother's home, right?

Thand's eyes narrowed as he looked at Oden. "What's going on?"

Oden didn't respond. Instead, he shouted an order. "You two men guard the boat. And you two, position yourselves close to the village but stay out of sight. You know the consequences if Lord Creedy finds us. Everyone stay alert."

The boys looked at the princess with questioning looks.

"Come on, we don't want to be seen. I'll explain at the house."

Avoiding the main path, they stayed in the shadows of the trees and moved quickly. Oden lagged behind, looking over his shoulder often. Grace was busy in the back garden when the four of them appeared. She stopped her digging, smiled, and began to express her happiness at seeing the princess again. But Eschon put a finger to his lip and pointed to the door.

Once inside, Grace looked at Thand and said, "Something's wrong. Tell me."

Thand shrugged his shoulders and tilted his head toward Princess Sharman. The princess looked at Grace and took a deep breath—asking this question had seemed easier to her last night.

"Will you allow Thand and Eschon to return with me to Adrianna Island? I would like them to meet my father, King Treutlen, and explain to him how Lord Creedy unfairly treats the good people of Elingale and forbids education. I also would like my father to hear how your way of life has improved since we've established a school. He could—"

Eschon was already shaking his head before the princess was halfway through her sentence.

"No. I'm not going *anywhere* on that big ship!"

"There's nothing to be afraid of," Oden said, looking amused. "It's like being at home once you get used to the motion."

"Not ever," Eschon cried again. "Besides, who's going to help Mother if I'm away? And what's Creedy going to do when he finds the princess missing? No. Thand is the best choice to go. He can answer all the questions. I'm needed here."

"I'm not so sure myself," Thand added. "Eschon is right about Creedy. He's dangerous when angered. Besides, I don't know how to talk to a king. Why would he even listen to someone like me? How will I get home again? Suppose we're attacked by the pirates? I'd like to help you, Princess, but I'm not sure I would be of any use."

"I understand your concern, but fear of the unknown is natural. A big ship, an unfamiliar place, awkwardness—that's what you're afraid of. Agree to come and my father will help us work out a plan that makes Lord Creedy afraid of us. Just think, we could defeat him and transform your fear into action."

Grace had listened patiently, not giving any indication of how she would answer. When the princess had finished speaking, Grace asked her sons to sit at the table. She remained standing. She looked from boy to boy, then leaned forward with her hands pressing on the table.

"Listen to me, sons. Elwins learning to read, black storms, the princess being kidnapped—things like these don't happen on our island. They're signs of profound change—a reshaping of our lives into something better. In the short time that Princess Sharman has been with us, Elingale has grown stronger and more independent. If she leaves now and we do nothing different, life on the island will return to the same routine and Creedy will win. We can't allow that to happen. Princess Sharman has been telling us in her own way that it's time we take control of our lives and leave our old ways behind."

Grace hesitated for a moment and took a deep breath, as if she had just made a hard decision. "The king will be more likely to understand the Elwins if he hears the story firsthand. Maybe he will agree to help us, and maybe not. But either way, we cannot let Lord Creedy continue to treat us like he owns us."

Grace turned to Princess Sharman. "But Eschon can't go. He must remain with me. How can I let both of my sons leave at the same time? It's too much to ask."

Then she turned and made strong eye contact with her oldest son. "This voyage could lead to an extraordinary change in our lives, Thand. If you are willing to make the trip, you have my blessing. But the choice is yours."

Thand walked around the table and took his mother's hand. "It frightens me to think of leaving you and Eschon and everything I know, but I agree that we can't let things return to the past. We've tried but failed to solve our own problems. The best hope is to get help from Adrianna Island. I'll go."

The cloud of tension vanished with his answer. Grace kissed Thand on his forehead.

Eschon walked over to his brother. "You're the most courageous person on this island. If only I could overcome my fear and get on that ship with you...I hope you're not too disappointed in me."

Princess Sharman spoke up before Thand could respond. "You don't give yourself enough credit, Eschon. Lord Creedy is going to be difficult, maybe even dangerous. You're brave to stay behind and protect your mother. You'll have to be the strong one and show the way because everyone on Lapis Lazuli will look to you for leadership. It's going to take courage to survive Lord Creedy's outrage."

"I hope I can do what's expected," Eschon said, still doubtful. "Come on, Thand. I'll help you pack. If I think too much about Creedy's reaction, I might get on that ship with you. And bring Mother, of course."

Oden knew that everyone would like a few moments to say goodbye, but he couldn't avoid the need for haste. "We don't have much time. You must hurry, Thand. The longer we stay on the island, the greater the danger. And we must be on the ship before the tide begins to rise."

"The sooner you get started, the sooner you'll return," Grace added, hiding the sadness in her heart.

Thand didn't own much, so packing was simple. He found a white canvas bag that had once contained mill-flour and turned it into a knapsack. Eschon added some of his own clothes when his brother wasn't looking.

A lump formed in Thand's throat, and he knew it was time to leave. He walked over to his mother and pressed her to his chest. He nearly squeezed the breath out of her before letting her go with a quick kiss. A tear leaked from his eye as he walked away.

Once outside, Eschon put his arm around his brother's shoulder and said, "Don't worry, kin. I'll take care of everything. Keep a journal of your adventure. I'll want to know everything that happened, and Scribe will want to add it to his history book. And cheer up; traveling with the princess can't be all bad."

The four of them walked to the beach without talking. The future was uncertain but conflict was for sure. Oden and Thand climbed into the longboat first. Princess Sharman squeezed Eschon's hand and kissed him on the cheek. He helped her climb in, then handed his brother the bag of clothes.

"Oden, look out for my brother—and Princess Sharman too."

Oden nodded approval to Eschon. "That's the plan."

Thand looked toward his brother and his throat constricted. This was more difficult than he'd imagined.

"Somehow I feel responsible for all of this suffering. I wish I could make it go away without leaving Elingale. But the remedy to the Black Storm is not here. You're strong, and I know you can help the villagers cope with Lord Creedy while I'm away. We'll all be better off when this is over. I'll miss you . . ."

Princess Sharman sensed that Thand was struggling with his emotions, so she reached down and held his hand for reassurance.

Oden seemed like he was about to get caught up in all the surrounding emotions when he saw his men watching him. He cleared his throat, put a scowl on his face, and shouted, "Look to the sea—row!"

Eschon stood alone, listening to the breaking waves. He watched as the boat shrank into the distance. A sad look, tinged with worry, showed on his face. For the first time in their lives, the boys were separated. Eschon was about to head back to the village when the sounds of barking dogs caught his attention.

"I'm surprised he didn't send them sooner," Eschon said to the fading boat. Then he turned and dashed toward the village.

Above, the fabled Kookachoo bird tilted its red wings and flew north.

Chapter 11

*L*ORD CREEDY UTTERED a soft curse as the last Elwin disappeared from his front lawn. He marched back inside, poured himself a strong drink, and sat down heavily. The heckling and insults rang in his ear, and his temples pulsed with anger as he recalled the image of rotten vegetables flying toward him. He took off his soiled shoes and threw them against the wall. Then he picked up his glass and hurled it at the door. It wasn't enough; he stood up, picked up his snake-cane, and slammed it into a flower vase. Shards flew in all directions, but he still wasn't satisfied. He moved around the room, swinging his cane while contemplating new ways to inflict punishment.

They threw rotten vegetables at me like I was a criminal on the road to execution, he thought. *They laughed at my offer of help. How dare they question me? All of those people would die from starvation if it weren't for me. The Elwins were happy until that so-called princess washed up on my island. She's the source of all these problems. I'll dispose of her tomorrow, and then everything will return to normal.*

Lord Creedy continued to pace the room, grinding his teeth, with vengeance on his mind. *I could drag her out to sea in a boat without food or water, but she's already shown she can survive that. A firing squad would work, but if her kingdom learned of how she died, they'd likely send an army.*

He stopped pacing and looked up at the ceiling as if he might find inspiration there. A black spider was silently spinning a web in the corner. *That's it; I'll have her dropped off in the area where that deadly spider, Mactabilis, lives. Anything that moves is food for that monster. Afterward, I'll bring her body back to the village. There won't be any doubt about how she died, and it will serve as an example of what I'll do to anyone else who defies me.*

Lord Creedy awoke in a terrible mood. Normally a meticulous dresser, he hastily clothed himself in black wool pants and a white linen shirt, then hurried to the kitchen. Just as he was sitting down to breakfast, an ashen-faced servant came running into the room, clutching his hands.

"Lord Creedy. The girl is missing from the cell."

"Missing? That's not possible."

"Your lord, when I unlocked the cell this morning, there was glass scattered everywhere and the bars on the window were gone. I have no idea how she did it."

"She didn't do it, you fool. Someone helped her escape. It must have happened last night, when the Elwins were keeping me busy at the front of the house. Get a search party together and take the tracking dogs. Start looking for her in the forest up north. She's probably hiding in the woods. Report back to me as soon as you know something. Now go!"

So, this is what last night was really about, Lord Creedy thought. *The Elwins are smarter than I thought. But still, they couldn't have done this without someone's help. But who? And where are they now?*

Lord Creedy rushed to the back of the mansion so that he could investigate for himself. He saw the steel bars lying on the ground and then went over to examine the window frame. At first, he thought that the Elwins must have chipped the mortar away from the steel bars. But when he looked closely, he could see the bars were bowed outward. Only something very strong could have done that. He thought about the tough little Elwins but concluded that they were not strong enough for such a feat. However, a horse would have the strength to pull the bars out of the wall. So he began to look for further evidence. About ten feet from the wall, he found hoof prints.

The Elwins have no horses, so they must have used mine, he thought.

He walked with deliberate steps toward the barn, head down and eyes scanning for more clues. *There, that footprint is too large for an Elwin.*

Myke was in the barn feeding the horses when he saw Lord Creedy walking toward the rear of the house. His stride was stiff and his fists were clenched. Anyone who knew Lord Creedy understood that look, and anyone who saw that look wanted to be somewhere else. It was time for Myke to disappear. He climbed the ladder quicker than a field mouse and dashed to the back of the loft where some loose hay had been piled. He dove for the center of the stack, burying himself deep, and then lay motionless while trying to control his breathing.

Lord Creedy rushed into the barn and called for Myke. No answer. He called again, then started searching the individual horse stalls. He picked up a nearby pitchfork and stabbed at a few hay piles.

"You can come out and talk, or I can starve your family. Your choice."

A few pieces of hay drifted down from the ceiling, and Creedy jabbed his fork between the slats, just missing Myke's leg. He took a step and jabbed again.

"Okay, I'll come and get you, you little runt."

A field worker came in waving his hands above his head. "Lord Creedy, come quick, a clue."

Creedy dropped the tool and ran outside to see his worker pointing at the path leading away from the barn.

"Horse tracks? Use your brain," he said, annoyed by the lack of reason. "They could've been made anytime. Keep looking."

Creedy walked back toward the barn, struggling to put the puzzle together. *I know the Elwins rescued her, but I can't believe that they did this on their own. If they were capable of breaking her out, the girl would've been rescued days ago. None of my workers would have had the nerve to help them, so that means help had to come from another place. That's it! Her country must have sent a search party and they stumbled into the Elwins. That would explain the Elwins' behavior last night. And considering this is an island, the search party would've had to come by way of a ship. That means someone came ashore at the beach and then helped her escape. I've been tricked; they're headed to the water, not the forest.*

Lord Creedy started running toward the house while yelling for his guards.

"Locate the search party. Tell them to come back to the barn and start tracking toward the sea. Hurry, they've already wasted too much time."

⊶——◆——⊷

It was late afternoon when the search party returned to the barn. Sweat stained their shirts and they appeared exhausted, but Lord Creedy was too annoyed to care.

"You call yourselves trackers? You're looking north when she went south, and by now she may be anywhere."

"But you told us to start up north, in the woods," a dog handler said. "I would've started around the busted window."

Astonished by the brash comment, Creedy struck the man alongside his head with the snake-cane. "You're a dunderhead and not capable of doing this job properly. Get off my island. Now! Everyone else goes back to searching. I want that girl back here by nightfall."

Shepherd, the lead tracker, was a tall, square-built man and was more self-assured than most of Creedy's workers. Lord Creedy's speech hadn't frightened him or changed the fact that the men and dogs were worn-out and hungry. His tracker was right—Creedy didn't know the first thing about this. And his men deserved a break. He knew of a nearby stream, away from spying eyes, where the men could cool off and drink as well as eat wild berries that grew along the bank. The hunting party had barely wet their lips when suddenly a twig snapped, the dogs barked, and a deer bolted away. Was someone following? Shepherd ordered the men to fill their pockets quickly and continue the hunt. The men grumbled but did as ordered.

The sun was all but set when the searchers arrived at the water's edge. One of the trackers began looking for clues on the beach while a second one scanned the horizon. A moment later he was leaping in the air and pointing to the sea.

"Look to the sea! There's a ship out there. Do you think the girl is on board? Maybe we can stop her."

Shepherd sighed heavily. "Look hard, you halfwit, and you'll see men climbing into the rigging. The tide is running out, and they'll be dropping the sails any minute. Unless you can run on water, the ship will be over the horizon in a short time."

Everyone was irritable and exhausted from the endless day of tracking. Murmured talk of giving up began but was quickly silenced by the howl of a hound. The baying sound sent a jolt of energy through Shepherd and re-energized the team. The dogs tugged on their leashes and corkscrewed their handlers through the undergrowth while barking a secret language. Without warning, the lead dog gave a mournful cry, turned sharply to the right, and almost yanked the tracker off of his feet. The man could scarcely stay on his feet as the dog sprinted down a path that led straight into Elingale.

The people of Elingale had heard the dogs barking long before the search party arrived. They thought Lord Creedy had sent his dogs to terrorize the village as repayment for last night's protest. Many locked themselves inside of their houses or ran in the opposite direction of the howling.

The excited animals dragged the men all through the village, tails wagging, nostrils flaring in and out. Their route was a series of short bursts to the right and cutbacks to the left, but when they reached a specific house, the dog's howling increased significantly. The pursuit had led to the front of Grace's house. Shepherd ordered two men to go around back and watch the rear door while he strode into the house. He carried a coil of rope on his hip and the strain of a long day on his face.

"Where's the girl?" asked Shepherd with an intimidating voice.

Grace had her arms crossed over her chest and gave the man a hard stare. "Why're you asking me? You're the ones who took her."

Len, another tracker, began to strike the palm of his hand with a short wooden club while looking Grace in the eyes. "You may not be familiar with Lord Creedy's justice. If you know what's good for you, you'll answer the question."

Eschon stepped toward the threatening man, but Grace put her arm out to stop him. Eschon glared at Len and then turned, walked over to the corner, and picked up a long, sharp blade that he normally used for cutting stalks. He moved toward the man who had threatened his mother. "We're not afraid of you."

"You better have a bigger weapon than that if you want to frighten me."

However, Len's shrill voice exposed his doubt. The tension was escalating fast, so Grace spoke up before the confrontation turned violent.

"I've got nothing to say to either of you, and if you bring Lord Creedy here, I'll tell him the same. Now, get out of here!"

Shepherd looked at the hostile boy and then back to his mother. He had thought intimidation would work, but now he was unsure. Furthermore, he didn't know how hard Creedy wanted him to push. After all, he was looking for the princess, not a village mother.

Shepherd made a disgusted snort, then leaned in toward Grace. "We both know who's going to win this argument. Come on, Len. It's time we get back to Lord Creedy with our report."

As Len walked out, he knocked over a flower vase and then looked back at Eschon, daring him to do something about it.

Eschon clenched his jaw, but out of respect for his mother, he waited for the men to leave. "Why did you stop me, Mother? He threatened you."

"Yes, but he was trying to provoke us. Starting a fight would've been a perfect reason for him to grab you and take you back to Lord Creedy. I'm not losing a second son today."

Lord Creedy was pushing away from the dinner table when the lead tracker arrived with his report. The man looked hungrily at the remaining food.

"Your clothes are filthy and you stink!" Creedy said, waving a hand in front of his face. "Don't ever show up at my dining table in this condition again. And I already know what you're going to say. I figured it out myself."

"Then I'll leave," said the leader, scarcely hiding his anger.

"I'll tell you when you are to leave," Creedy barked. "Now, tell me what you've discovered."

Shepherd stiffened and ground his teeth, trying to regain control of his emotions. "As you already know, the search for the girl leads to the water's edge. A three-mast ship was setting its sails when we arrived. Almost certainly the girl was aboard. The dog's picked up a secondary trail that led back to Elingale and to a specific house, probably the house where she lived while playing teacher. I talked to the woman inside, and she was very arrogant; her son had a similar attitude. My guess is the lady knows more than anyone else in the village, but it's going to take more than a verbal threat to make her talk."

Lord Creedy gave an arrogant laugh. "I can do better than a verbal threat. Bring her here tomorrow, and I'll show you how tight-lipped she is."

The sounds of a blacksmith hammering steel woke Lord Creedy in the morning. He had an upset stomach and was still troubled that he had been outfoxed by the Elwins. After a simple breakfast of bread and watered wine, the lord headed outside to check on the repair work being done on his dungeon window. He talked to the blacksmith first.

"I want these bars twice as thick as the old ones and four inches longer. No one's ever going to escape that room again."

"I'll have them ready by early afternoon," the smithy hollered above the clanging.

"No later, or you'll spend tomorrow looking at those bars from a different perspective."

The man stopped his hammering and looked Lord Creedy in the eyes. "I said it will be done."

Lord Creedy walked away, happy to distance himself from the fierce heat of the forge. The sound of pounding began anew, and he headed for his next stop—the mason.

"I want those bars cemented into the window so that the walls will fall down before the bars pull out."

Without looking up, the mason continued chipping in the center of the stone. "I have two more stones to make ready. Then I'll set the bars in the holes and mortar everything to the wall. No one will ever escape through that window again. I'll bet my life on it."

"You just did."

It had been three days since the girl had escaped, and it was time for the Elwins to pay for their actions. Creedy wanted the villagers to be reminded of what happens to anyone who attempts to defy him, so he sent the same two men and coach he'd used for kidnapping the princess. Six extra horsemen were added to make sure his plan succeeded.

Creedy's men galloped into Elingale just after noon on the only day the Elwins were allowed to rest. The coach rolled into the village and made a slow circle around the town square, while the riders chased down anyone on the street, rearing their horses back at the last minute. The carriage pulled to a stop outside Grace's house, and the horsemen surrounded the building.

Grace had seen the parade of men prancing through Elingale, intimidating the villagers. She knew the next few minutes would be dangerous. So she made Eschon promise not to interfere, and she waited just inside the door with her arms crossed.

Shiny stepped out of the coach, his muscles straining the buttons on his white shirt. A rider dressed in a black hooded cape scanned the crowd and then dismounted. Together, they walked to Grace's house and entered—uninvited.

Grace raised her hands into a blocking position. "No one invited you in."

"We're not looking for an invitation," said the man in black. "In fact, we're not even here to have a talk. Just step outside and get in that coach. And don't put on a show like the teacher girl."

"Where's Lord Creedy?" asked Grace. "Is he afraid to come to the village and talk? Is he afraid of the jeers he might hear?"

"Get in the coach," Shiny said with bared teeth.

Grace walked up to Shiny and then shoved him aside. "Don't threaten me, baldy. I'll go. Not because you frighten me, but because it's best for the village."

Lord Creedy had badgered and threatened Grace for over an hour, and still she remained tight-lipped. He decided a softer approach might work on a woman.

"I don't understand. Why have the Elwins turned against me? I always made sure you had work and food. What else could you want?"

Grace choked back a laugh but continued to stare at him like he was insane.

When she didn't give a reply, he said, "Well, things have returned to normal. No princess, no teaching, and no more problems. But I sense there is more to this story. And until I know everything that has taken place—including who helped your princess escape—you'll be our guest in my newly reconstructed dungeon. When you're ready to talk, call the guard."

Chapter 12

T HE EVENTIDE WAS rising as they boarded the ship. Oden held the longboat steady while Princess Sharman took his hand and climbed out. When her feet hit the deck, Oden exhaled an audible sigh of relief.

"We finally have you back to stay," he said, embracing her warmly. "It's been difficult for everyone, especially you, but soon you'll be home with your family. Let's hope for fair winds and a calm sea."

"Thank you, Oden," the princess said and rose up on her tip-toes to place a kiss on his cheek. Oden squeezed her hand, then turned toward the front of the ship.

The remaining sailors exited quickly, leaving Thand sitting alone and confused. Feeling like a castaway, he climbed out of the longboat and tumbled onto the deck. He stood up, face flushed from embarrassment, then reached back into the boat for his sack of clothes. He looked across the deck. *Now what? Where do I go?* Then he spotted Oden walking away from the princess. He called to her and waved, but she didn't seem to notice. Sprinting across the deck, dodging sailors, and nearly tripping over a rope, he reached her just as she put her hand on a door latch.

Thand's face was taut, his voice strained. "What now? Where do we go?"

"Sorry, Thand, I can't talk now. Before I left the ship this morning, the captain told me, 'Report to me as soon as your land-loving legs hit the deck.' I have to go. I'll see you later."

Thand was left standing alone, staring at the great ship, looking at all the ropes and sails. His first thought was to jump overboard and swim home. Then he closed his eyes. *I have to overcome this fear of the unknown.* He could hear his father's words: "If you ever get lost, look at your surroundings, recognize the differences, and then make them seem familiar. A path will open up."

Okay, the smells of canvas and damp wood are different, but the salt-tinged air is the same. The sailors' talk is unfamiliar, but I don't need to learn all the details of a ship. The swaying motion of the ship will take getting used to, but the sound of waves is familiar. He took deep breaths of the cool night air. His heartbeat slowed as he gained confidence.

Thand opened his eyes, and at once the ship felt different—powerful but unthreatening, methodical not chaotic. His earlier fears were replaced by a strong desire to investigate and learn more. He walked toward the center of the ship, trying to understand how something this big was able to move through the water with such speed. Thand saw a barefoot boy wearing tattered green pants with a red-and-white striped shirt walking straight toward him. He was a little shorter than Thand, with straw-colored hair and a pimpled face. The deckhand introduced himself as Brevis and requested Thand to follow him. They walked across the wooden deck, sidestepping men, while Thand asked simple questions.

"Your worries tell me you're a landlubber, so for now I'll give you the basics. The object that looks like a tree in the center of the ship is the mainmast, and it's the tallest of the three. The one toward the bow, the front, is the foremast. And the aft, or rear to you, is the mizzenmast, and it's also the shortest. The arms holding the sails are called yards. The basket at the top is the highest part of the ship, and it's used as a lookout, to spot land or other ships. We call it the crow's nest. Watch your head."

They came to a short door that opened to a companionway. Brevis led the way down the ladder and into a narrow passageway, where new aromas assaulted Thand's senses.

"What are all of those different smells?"

"Well, friend, that's our ship's own lovely fragrance—sweaty sailors, damp canvas, exotic spices, and some others that you really don't want to know about. Pick whichever smell you like."

"Not much of a choice."

"Well, tonight we'll add sour wine and stale beer."

"Fresh air would be my pick."

"Then you'll be spending most of your time on deck. First door on the left is your quarters. The captain must like you if he gave you your own room. Now you won't have to sleep next to snoring men who reek of rum and sweat."

The cabin door creaked open from the movement of the ship. Thand pointed to something that looked like a fishing net hanging between the walls. "What's that?"

"It's called a hammock and you sleep in it. It's more comfortable than it looks. The hammock swings so the motion of the ship won't toss you on the floor."

The cabin boy gave a demonstration, but Thand still wasn't sure of its usefulness. It looked more like a caterpillar's nest than a bed. Brevis patted Thand on his back. "You'll get it soon enough."

Thand thanked the boy as he left, then stowed his meager belongings in a corner. There wasn't a window in the room—only an oil lamp—so it didn't take long for Thand to feel like he'd been locked inside a box. He looked at the hammock and decided to give it a try.

It looks like a fish net, he thought. *Well let's see what it's like to be the fish.*

He sat on the thick, cord-lined edge and then leaned back but in a single swift motion the hammock just flipped him out the other side. Thand chuckled as he got off the floor and tried again. After several more ejections, he got it right. Now, lying on his back, nursing a bruised elbow, he began to reflect on his decision to leave home. *So far, I've been ignored and left to fend for myself.* Thand scowled at the ceiling. *This was not what I expected.* The air was growing stale and his anxiety was increasing. *I need to find Princess Sharman and be reminded why this was a good idea.*

He shifted to get out of the hammock and, again, was flipped onto the floor. *This is growing old,* he thought as he got up. Then, forgetting how low the ceiling was, he bumped his head on the oil lamp. It was definitely time to track down the princess.

Thand stood on deck and filled his lungs with fresh air. He had a ways to go before the smelly, cramped quarters became routine. A clanking sound from the front of the ship caught his attention. *Bow,* he corrected. Sailors were walking in a circle, pushing handgrips that turned a cogwheel that lifted the heavy sea anchor. A tall, sturdy man, who Thand guessed was the captain, stood above everyone. He was wearing a blue jacket trimmed in red over matching blue trousers with a similar stripe. His furrowed face was covered by a well-groomed, white beard and a bristly, black moustache. Unlike many of the barefoot sailors, he wore black leather boots that nearly touched his knees. A wool cap with an emblem topped his hairless head.

The captain looked toward the top of the ship and shouted,

"Lay aloft and loose all sail." Along the yardarms, men untied the sails and let them fall. "Stand by to set sails," he said. Then, "Set the staysails." Each command began a flurry of well-coordinated activity that eventually led to all sails being trimmed. Now the wind could be harnessed to put Trident Seas' massive bulk in motion. The sails billowed, and a sudden pitch in the deck caused Thand to grab the rail.

There's no turning back. I'm really leaving my family behind and beginning a new chapter of my life.

Princess Sharman arrived at the captain's quarters just as he was pushing his chair back.

"Good, ya're here. Now, try to stay out of trouble. I have a ship to run." He sidestepped the princess and was gone.

Her surprise changed to a smile when he closed the door. *Good. Now I won't have to listen to a lecture on all the dangers of living on a ship.*

She dashed out and escaped to her cabin. Her quarters weren't as lavish as they'd been on Odyssey, but at least she had a small window and a desk. She opened her sea chest and pulled out her pen and ink. The time seemed good to begin a journal.

An hour had passed by when the cabin boy knocked on Princess Sharman's door. She put her writing materials away, then let him in. He was delivering a simple meal of biscuits and ale. An apple had been added as an acknowledgement of her royalty. The princess asked if all was well. Brevis informed her that Thand was in his cabin feeling seasick and that otherwise, all was normal. The princess finished her meal and then left in search of fresh air. Once on deck, she walked to the portside railing, glanced over the side of the ship, and watched the foamy white waves pass by. She took a deep breath of the fresh sea air, held it in her lungs, and then slowly exhaled. There was something about the pleasant smell of the ocean that made this a universal habit.

The waves were gently rolling, and the wind was barely a breeze. A waxing moon hung in the nighttime sky, casting an orange luster across the water. The princess was admiring the view when Thand walked up and leaned on the rail next to her. His stomach had improved, as well as his mood. He followed her gaze out to sea.

"This is beautiful. Maybe I made the right decision to leave home. Tell me about your island. What makes it a nicer place?"

"Adrianna's natural beauty isn't very different from Lapis Lazuli. The big difference is that my kingdom allows people to make choices in their occupations—like becoming craftsmen or laborers. If they don't want to work in the fields, they can learn specialized skills and become carpenters or blacksmiths, maybe bakers or fishmongers. Because of this concept, Adrianna Island has a greater supply of food, sturdier houses, and easier ways to travel. Someday, if we prevail over Lord Creedy, Lapis Lazuli may be similar."

"What about other places?"

"The world is vast, and there is an endless amount to see and learn. Exploring will give you the chance to meet other people and learn about new lands. For example, if you were to venture far over the horizon, you would find animals that are as tall as a tree or the size of a house. You'd find birds and flowers that come in more sizes and colors than you can imagine. You'd find new foods with distinctive aromas and textures."

His eyebrows rose. "What else?"

"If you travel far enough, you'll see that weather affects the clothes people wear and the types of houses they live in. I've read about mountains so high they touch the sky and temperatures so cold the rain turns into a white powder called snow."

Thand closed his eyes and considered the possibilities. "I'd like to see the whole world."

"You'll never be able to do that, but you can better understand the world through reading books. Likewise, if you write down your experiences from this trip, then the Elwins can discover what it was like to be with us."

A wide grin formed on Thand's face. "Wouldn't it be great to share this with Eschon and Mother and all my friends? Maybe you can help me write about our voyage when it's over."

"I'll help, but you have to write it in your own words."

Thand realized that he would have to learn many new words to describe this story. Then, looking up at the tall mast and the orange canvas sails reflecting the moonlight, he continued, "It's hard to believe that wind is the only thing making this ship move."

"Yes, but speaking of wind, tell me about the thunderstorm. I heard Oden say something about a black storm, but I didn't know what he was referring to."

"Eschon said the storm formed so fast that no one saw it coming. It began with a dust storm, and then the wind, rain, and lightning attacked them like a mad army. A young boy almost died. I was at the mill, but the storm remained south and didn't affect me. That's probably why I'm the only one who can still read."

For a moment, the princess had a blank look on her face. "What are you talking about? You're the only one who can read?"

He described the storm in more detail and then told her that everyone had lost the ability to read.

"That's impossible! How could a storm destroy all of the hard work that we did?"

"I don't know, but I'm sure Lord Creedy had a hand in it."

Oden had walked over while they were talking. After a few minutes of listening, he spoke up.

"Eschon told me about the featherlight dust and the sizzle of the lightning bolts. All of which makes me wonder if the storm was a distraction to mask some type of evil magic."

"Evil magic, Black Storms—this makes it all the more important that you meet my father. Oden, I've heard rumors of a very powerful wizard who lives in the mountains of Adrianna Island."

"He's no rumor," Oden replied. "The wizard and your father worked together to rid Adrianna Island of vicious traitors many years ago. They're the reason we live in peace and have prospered since that time."

"You know him? Then you can go with us and ask the wizard for his help."

"A meeting with the wizard is not that simple. The trip to his castle is difficult and filled with danger. It's not to be taken lightly."

"We're not afraid, are we, Thand?"

"No! Well, maybe a little."

"It doesn't matter. Only your father can make that decision," Oden said firmly. "I'm sorry, I have other duties to complete. But we can talk later."

Thand was settling into life aboard the ship. The smell of the sea and the sound of the waves breaking on the bow now seemed ordinary. Brevis had taught him to flex his knees, absorbing the motion of the ship, and nowadays, walking on the rising and falling deck seemed as natural as breathing. One of the sailors had told him that he'd at last gotten his "sea legs."

It was just past high noon when Thand found Princess Sharman's room. He knocked on the door and entered. She was sitting at the desk with one hand on her chin while tapping a pen against her journal. The blank look disappeared as her posture straightened.

"I'm glad you're here. I've been thinking about the day of the Black Storm. Did anything strange happen to *you*?"

"I did see the Kookachoo Bird."

She chuckled at the name. "What's that?"

"The Kookachoo Bird is a very mysterious bird. Most people have never seen one. It appears only in times of great change. At least, that's what the legend says."

"I've never heard of this bird, but the legend sounds interesting. Tell me the story."

Thand flapped his arms like a bird. *"Koo-kook-a-choo, koo-kook-a-choo.* That's the sound of the bird call."

"Well, it sounds appropriate. I hope the legend is as interesting as the name."

Thand smiled. Now it was his chance to explain something extraordinary.

"On the afternoon of the storm, I was riding back from the mill, not paying much attention to the road, when I saw a red bird land in a nearby tree. The bird looked at me and tilted its head. It seemed to be evaluating or judging me to see if I was the appropriate person. I returned the inquisitive stare and impulsively asked for its white feather."

"Why would you ask for a feather?"

"All the feathers of the Kookachoo Bird are a bright red, like the color of a cardinal. However, there is a single white feather in the center of its tail that's much longer than the others. It's said that the person who finds the Kookachoo's white feather will be blessed with good luck and fortune. It is also said that there are hidden powers that reside within the feather."

"That's intriguing. The feather must be very valuable."

"Yes, it's sought by many. They hope it will increase their wealth and drive their enemies away."

"I bet rulers would pay a sizable amount of money to own that feather."

"Yes, but you can't just buy the feather. According to the legend, if you were to kill the bird for its feather, the magic would be lost. Also, if the white feather is stolen or taken by force from the legitimate owner, the power of the feather ceases, and it becomes just another pretty ornament, useless to the thief."

"But the fact that you saw the Kookachoo means something is about to change?"

"Yes, if the legend is true. But change for who, and what kind?"

The princess's eyes gleamed with possibilities. "I'm not sure, but it's exciting to think about what may happen. I am going to see this as a good omen."

<hr />

The soft morning light had faded into an azure sky by the time Thand went on deck. He was expecting to find Oden, but a shout from the crow's nest announced land ahead—Adrianna Island. Instantly, the ship became more energized. The words were welcomed news for the sailors, who had not laid eyes on home for several months. Good-natured jostling, singing, and humming added to the air of excitement.

The Trident Seas turned smoothly into the mouth of a large river. Sailors lined the yardarms, waiting for orders. The captain was wearing his usual crisp blue jacket and polished boots. Just before the waterway narrowed, he ordered the sails to be dropped, slowing the ship's speed. As they progressed farther up the river, expansive fields of grain filled the port side and willow trees lined the banks. The willow branches swayed on the light breeze, as if they were waving greetings to the returning ship.

The town coasted into sight, and the muddy riverbank was replaced with a low stone wall. Scanning ahead, Thand saw black-and-white, half-timbered structures sitting shoulder to shoulder. The top floor of several buildings extended beyond the ground walls, creating an overhang. Shops with large windows occupied the first floor of many buildings, while families lived above. Along the harbor wall, children sat upon their fathers' shoulders, squealing and pointing, while countless others waved cheerfully to the returning ship. Thand was still gaping at the strange sights when a sailor pushed him to one side.

"Stand aside," the mariner barked as he heaved a heavy rope to a man on the landing pier.

Princess Sharman walked up behind Thand. "Welcome to Empeerean, the most important city on Adrianna Island. Stay out of the men's way until the ship's docked, then you can follow me."

As he turned toward the sound of the princess's voice, Thand's mouth fell open. The princess was dressed in a long, green silk garment with white pearl buttons cascading down the front. A black hooded cape lined in crimson velvet was draped over her shoulders and fastened by a silver clasp.

"Where did that come from?"

"My mother, the optimist, wanted me to look proper when I returned home. She stowed a separate trunk in the captain's cabin before the ship departed Adrianna."

The dress flared as she spun around in a circle. "Do you approve?"

"Well, I still like the blue one with seaweed, but this one is suitable," he teased.

The upgrade in her clothing made Thand think about his own appearance. A thigh-length tunic of brown wool over his drab trousers and simple, laced-up leather boots was meager in comparison. Just as he looked up from his shoes, Princess Sharman took hold of his hand and guided him down the narrow gangplank. The king's guards were standing on either side of the ramp, waiting to welcome her. Their uniforms consisted of royal-blue surcoats worn over white-colored stockings. Some had broadswords, with golden hilts, fastened to their hips. In their left hands, the soldiers clutched green metal shields painted with the royal emblem—a lion facing a unicorn. Their right hands were kept free for swinging their weapons. Soldiers without shields gripped long, polished lances topped with ax heads. All wore polished steel helmets festooned with black crests made of horsehair.

Thand was intimidated by the presence of the armored men. He walked through their icy stares, staying close to the princess. At the end of the dual column, a beautifully decorated, red-and-gold carriage was waiting. Four white horses were hitched and ready to transport the princess back to the palace. The driver bowed as he opened the coach door. He reached inside, pulled down a folding step, and motioned for the princess to climb inside. When Thand moved toward the coach, the man blocked his way and told him to follow in the baggage wagon.

Princess Sharman shook her finger in front of the driver's face. "Don't be rude. He goes in my coach, with me."

The driver's cheeks flushed crimson as he pulled on his collar. "As you wish, my lady."

Thand gawked at the extravagant interior instead of watching his step. He stumbled and collapsed into the lap of the princess, causing an audible gasp from the crowd. Princess Sharman behaved as if this were a normal occurrence and told Thand to take the seat across from her. He looked at the door handle, contemplating a run for the ship, but the princess put her hand over his and gave it a squeeze.

Once the carriage began to move, Thand raised his head and looked out the window. His eyes widened as he momentarily forgot his embarrassment. There were so many unfamiliar sights that he couldn't begin to guess. The princess recognized the wonder in his eyes and moved closer, pointing out features of the city.

"The shop with the loaves of bread in the window is the baker's shop. Doesn't it smell wonderful? Over there is our marketplace where fruits and vegetables are sold, and next to them is a seller of soap and candles. The booth with the meat hanging from the crossbar is a butcher's stall."

"Why is all of this displayed outside?"

"So people can see what's available to purchase."

Thand's eyebrows rose. "You mean they have more than they need for themselves?"

"Yes. When a worker produces more than is required, he can sell the remainder to others. On Lapis Lazuli, Lord Creedy keeps the surplus, leaving nothing for the Elwins to sell. He ships it to traders and retains the profit for his own use. I hope we can change that so one of these days Elingale will have its own marketplace."

It was understandable that Thand didn't comprehend commerce, so she went back to describing the city.

"Look, that two-story building is a tavern. They sell food and drink on the ground floor, and travelers can spend the night in the rooms upstairs. The clanging sound you hear is coming from a blacksmith shop that is behind the inn."

Thand kept silent, but thought of Princess Sharman's words from earlier: *There's an incredible amount to discover.*

They rode past several farms before passing into a cheerless forest where menacing tree branches reached down in a threatening fashion. At the first mile marker, the road split and the carriage swung left. Immediately, the makeup of the road changed. They entered into a long tunnel lit by soft green light. Thand thought something magical had happened but soon realized the trees had been trimmed to form an arch of green leaves. A hundred yards down the lane, the carriage exited the tunnel. Without warning, Princess Sharman squealed and grabbed Thand's hand.

"Look up there! That's where I live."

The castle was situated on the crest of a high knoll. Up ahead, a wide wooden bridge crossed a serpentine river that wandered along the base of the hilltop. Two stone lions, resting on marble bases, guarded the bridge. Against a cloudless sky, six blue-tiled turrets could be seen rising above the gleaming white walls. Over the arched entrance, banners gently rippled in the breeze.

The horses clopped across the bridge, and as soon as the carriage passed through the alabaster walls, trumpets blared. The horses came to a stop in front of the Great Hall, where a steward was waiting patiently. He opened the carriage door with one gloved hand and smoothly offered the other to help the princess exit. Thand followed along, tugging on his clothes while giving sidelong glances. Again, he wished he owned finer clothes, and he began to understand why Lord Creedy had so many choices in his wardrobe. They ascended a wide marble staircase and entered a grand room. Family and friends waited eagerly to greet Princess Sharman. Hugs and kisses were spread around generously, and a considerable fuss was made over the long-absent princess.

Immediately, Thand felt cut off, like a bridge over water had collapsed and he couldn't swim to the other side. It was an unexpected feeling and one that he didn't like. How was it possible that he could feel so alone in a crowd of people? With no hope of rejoining the princess, he moved to a corner and studied the sea of people. Some wore gowns made of soft fabric; others wore gowns that were smooth and shiny. All were decorated with many shiny baubles. Thand began to think that the more extravagantly a person dressed, the greater his or her power. The queen's dress had the highest amount of detail and decorative stitching. She also wore more jewelry than anyone else in the room, which seemed to prove his point.

When the excitement began to subside, the princess saw Thand standing backed against a wall, rubbing one arm and looking around. She hurried over to Thand's side and apologized.

"It was never my intention to leave you alone. The crowd overwhelmed me. I'm sorry."

"You seem very popular," Thand said and accepted her explanation.

"I know how you feel right now—lost and overwhelmed. It's the same reaction I had on the first day we met. Hopefully neither of us will feel this way again."

"I'll be okay," said Thand unconvincingly.

"Let me introduce you to my mother, Queen Twila."

The queen was shorter than Princess Sharman, slightly round, and broad-hipped. Her silver hair, piled high on her head, made her look taller than Thand. The queen reached out her hand and touched Thand's cheek, making him feel truly welcome for the first time that day. He knew at once where Princess Sharman's warm and caring personality came from.

"I am pleased to make your acquaintance," she said generously. "I do not know the full reason for your presence here with my daughter, but I do know that you played a significant role in returning her safely to us. You will always be welcome in our kingdom."

Turning back to Princess Sharman, she said, "Your father would like to see you. You may take this young man with you and introduce him to the king. I will talk to you later, and then you may give me the details of your journey."

Princess Sharman took Thand by the hand and led him down a long corridor. Tall windows lined one side of the hall, and vases of fresh flowers sat on top of black marble pedestals. Mirrors hung opposite the windows and reflected the light and beauty of the outside gardens. Oil portraits of men in armor and ladies in beautifully flowing gowns were hung along the wall.

Thand stopped and looked up at a crystal chandelier. "I wish that Eschon was here to see all of this."

A pair of huge oak doors with shining brass handles waited at the end of the long corridor. Flanking the entrance were two soldiers clothed in red-and-gold uniforms with lances at their sides. They appeared to stare straight ahead; yet, their penetrating eyes allowed nothing to escape their notice. They were suspicious of the wiry man on the left but quickly recognized Princess Sharman. They cried out, "Danu," her childhood name that means queen of goodness. Seeing their princess alive and in good health filled them with happiness. Broad smiles cracked their faces; however, the guards quickly regained their composure, bowed to her, and then came back to attention. Without saying another word, they opened the heavy doors. Princess Sharman smiled affectionately, then touched each man on his cheek before leading Thand into the King's Hall.

The hall was a massive chamber surrounded by gleaming white marble walls. Banners hung from the lofty ceiling, while shields and coats of arms lined the sidewalls. Columns with gold-plated tops rose thirty feet to support a minstrel's gallery along one side of the hall. A long red carpet ran down the middle of the room and ended at the foot of several raised steps that rose to make a pyramid-shaped platform. Atop the dais sat the king's throne, which was made of gold and padded with red velvet. Behind the throne was a very large tapestry of the king's seal. It was a field of green silk, stitched with gold thread, depicting the bodies of a lion and a unicorn challenging each other.

Upon the throne sat King Treutlen. When he saw his daughter, the tall, rusty-haired man stood, and the room became silent. A broad smile crossed his whiskery face as he held out both arms and motioned for his daughter to come forward. The princess stopped at the base of the dais, curtseyed, and then, forgetting all formal custom, ran excitedly up the steps to her father.

"My precious Princess, you have returned to me," said the king, squeezing his only daughter until he thought she would break. He stood back, his strong arms resting on her shoulders as he looked at her. "You don't seem to be harmed, though it looks like you have grown more beautiful since I last saw you."

The princess put her face against his chest and locked her arms around his waist. "I am fine. But I'm worried about Uncle Warmund. Is he safe? Has he returned home?"

King Treutlen pinched the bridge of his nose and closed his eyes. "There's no news. However, a ship is continuing to search for him. We hope they will return soon with your uncle on board—just as Trident Seas returned with you."

She dropped her hands to her side as she sighed. Her father squeezed her shoulders, then told her not to be troubled. But secretly he was suffering. Warmund was his only brother and he'd been gone too long. The king put the thought away; today was a happy day. Then, with a kingly smile, he looked at Thand.

"Is this the young man who helped you through your ordeal?"

The princess put aside her worry and beckoned Thand to come forward.

"This is Thand from Lapis Lazuli Island. He and his brother rescued me from the sea. Thand, this is my father, King Treutlen, Good Ruler of Adrianna Island."

Thand had been in a daze since arriving on the island, and the effect had only increased as the day had worn on. He'd never realized that such opulence existed, and he'd certainly never envisioned Princess Sharman living this way. Thand had considered her a beautiful girl who had washed up on their beach in a wet dress. He had never visualized her as a *real* princess from a *real* kingdom. He was overwhelmed and didn't know how to respond to the king. The young Elwin half-bowed, then stuck out his hand as if to shake, pulled it back, and finally kneeled down and turned crimson red. He seemed to be making a habit of embarrassing himself.

"Thand, please rise. We're not as formal as you may think. Thank you for assisting my daughter. Your bravery will not go unrewarded."

Thand rose hesitantly, looked at the princess, then at the king, and finally said, "Please, sir, the only reward I hope for is help restoring our ability to read and write."

"Forgive me," the king said, rubbing his chin. "I haven't been made aware of the reason for your visit. I have interrupted this assembly and must continue. I'll meet with Oden afterward, and he'll inform me of your history. We will meet again before the day ends."

Princess Sharman knew they had been dismissed. She kissed

her father's fuzzy cheek. Then she pulled on Thand's hand and began to lead him out of King's Hall. Thand was still awestruck, looking from side to side, then up at the elaborate ceiling. Unintentionally, he stepped on Princess Sharman's heel, causing her to stumble and fall. Thand's own reaction was slow, and he fell on top of her, to the sound of horrified gasps.

The princess jumped to her feet with a flourish and saved the moment by saying, "And for our next act, I'll make Thand disappear."

Thand stood up, his face now the same color as the carpet. Afraid of every movement now, he looked at the runner in front of him as if it was a narrow bridge crossing a deep chasm. Then, like a duckling walking behind its mother, he followed the princess out of King's Hall.

Chapter 13

A MEETING OF COUNCILMEN was held that afternoon. As soon as a few administrative items were concluded, King Treutlen asked Oden to come forward and recount his daughter's ordeal. During the conversation, the king's face contorted many times. His brow wrinkled and his nostrils flared as each new segment was told. Oden spoke of the fate of Odyssey, the twice-rescue of his daughter, and her teaching efforts. The council also learned that schools were forbidden by the landowner and that a supernatural storm was thought to have wiped out the Elwins' ability to read.

Out of the corners of his eyes, the king watched the council react. A few looked bored and unfocused; others frowned or nodded in agreement. When the story came to an end, the king invited comments. Several councilmen advised that Adrianna Island should send the Elwins a ship loaded with goods as thanks for giving aid to the princess.

Then a very portly councilor stood up, brushing crumbs from the front of his black, embroidered doublet, and spoke. "I recommend we do nothing. After all, the Elwins are of no consequence to our kingdom. Why should we care about those little people? A shipload of goods is expensive."

Another man, thin and anxious, seemed worried about the

supernatural Black Storm: "A wizard with considerable skills would be needed. Maybe we shouldn't get involved."

King Treutlen's face tightened when he heard the last two comments. He stood, making eye contact with each advisor who had counseled him to do nothing.

"The Elwins have defied the lord of the manor while rescuing my daughter. Their attempt to improve their lives has been destroyed by a magical storm crafted by him. It is certain that Lord Creedy will punish the Elwins severely for freeing our princess. They did not turn their back on Princess Sharman's needs, and I won't abandon them. We will find an antidote to the wicked magic and then return to help the Elwins vanquish this tyrant."

While the meeting was being held, Princess Sharman led Thand to the kitchen. The cook was aware of the tasteless food served at sea, and she had laid out a sumptuous meal of minted lamb, garden vegetables, hot bread, and dates soaked in honey. As if that wasn't enough, an assortment of tortes and pies followed the main course. Thand backed away from the table, feeling like a puffer fish.

The princess patted her stomach, saying, "I feel like a stuffed pheasant. Let me show you the palace grounds. The walk will help us digest this extravagant feast."

Thand and Princess Sharman walked along another grand hallway filled with fine furnishings and more portraits of people Thand didn't know. The princess pointed out the library, the banquet hall, and the music room, but Thand said he had seen enough of fixtures and paintings.

They stepped outside and walked to the edge of the veranda.

Thand glanced around, then asked, "Why is there a wall around your palace?"

"It protects the people inside from assaults and gives a height advantage to our defenders."

"Why does the top of the wall look like it has missing teeth?"

The princess smiled at the comparison. "It's called crenellation. It allows the archers to stand sheltered behind the taller wall to notch their bows and then, when ready, shoot at the enemy from the gap."

They climbed a flight of steps and walked along the walls while Thand asked questions about the towers, the gates, and the moat. Eventually, he was satisfied with his exploration, and Princess Sharman guided him to an area where she was more comfortable. They strolled past a mounded hill of yellow flowers and green clover that was designed to look like the royal seal. A footpath, bordered by pink and white roses, led to a water pond. Centered in the pond was a statue of a lady pouring water from a jug.

Thand stopped and stared at the statue, then asked, "Why doesn't the jug run out of water?"

Princess Sharman said, "A man from a faraway city called Tivoli had something to do with its design, but I don't understand how it works. Something about water basins and pressure, but I'm not really sure."

As they moved past the pouring statue, Princess Sharman maneuvered Thand to an opening in the tall, cropped hedge where a stone bench sat in a recess. She told him to sit, then took his hand.

"This is a favorite spot of mine. On a sunny day, like today, I come here to reflect or maybe to write in my journal."

The view was pastoral. A perfectly manicured lawn sloped down to a small mirror-like lake, where several white swans glided silently across the still water, leaving a gentle ripple. Thand could have stayed there all day, but the princess had more to show him. She stood and motioned for him to follow.

As they walked the descending path to the lake, Thand asked, "Why did you leave all of this to travel? Isn't everything that you could ever want already here?"

"Yes, but to be thankful for what you have, you sometimes have to leave it. People who've never traveled think the entire world looks like their own and that everyone's manner of living is similar—but, as you've already seen, that's not true. If I hadn't chanced upon you and Eschon, I would've never been aware of Lapis Lazuli, or the Elwins, or you."

"But we did and I'm glad."

She smiled and nodded her agreement. "Let's go to the palace library, and I'll show you my favorite book. It's about a mouse that traveled the world while hiding in a ship. The library is peaceful, and we won't be disturbed. The silence allows your mind to expand and makes the books come alive."

It was late afternoon when the king asked that his daughter and guest be summoned to the council room. They arrived smiling; after all, they had just been on a journey around the world. When the king asked Thand to stand and explain the purpose of his visit, his smiled disappeared. He cleared his throat and then explained that Princess Sharman had convinced him to come and seek help. Thand described how the princess had improved the Elwins' lives by teaching them to read and write. He provided some examples that seemed minor to the council but were major to the Elwins. He ignored a snicker and explained that once Lord Creedy had become aware of their progress, he'd captured the princess. A few days later the Black Storm had materialized and destroyed all that they had learned.

The king nodded, and Princess Sharman told her story. Her pulse quickened when she described her capture and treatment—and how she was sure Lord Creedy had been punishing her for educating the Elwins. She agreed with Thand that these events were no coincidence, but additional brute force and magic would be needed to help the Elwins.

"It sounds as if you already have a plan in mind," said the king.

"I know there is a wizard living on Adrianna Island."

"There is. His name is Enunciation and he lives on Aerie Mountain. The fortress is built on an overhang that looks down into Mystic Valley, several miles below. The journey there is treacherous and exhausting."

"I'm not afraid," the princess said, displaying confidence.

"There are many places," the king continued, unyielding, "where the road is so narrow that men have fallen to their deaths. Savage wolves live on the mountain, and banshees haunt the night."

"I still want to meet the wizard."

King Treutlen was shaking his head as if the princess hadn't understood a single word. "It's too dangerous for you. But if you think it's necessary to seek the wizard's help, I'll send Oden and his soldier. If Thand wants to volunteer, he may go, but you're staying with me."

The princess's fists clenched. Her chin set high. "No, Father. I *will not* stay here. I am not afraid of the journey. I survived a pirate attack, had no food or water while floating on a sea chest, and was attacked by sharks. How could a trip through the mountains with experienced men be more difficult? I feel I owe it to the

Elwins. They helped me when I was in peril, and I am responsible for the Black Storm. It's my duty to—"

"Wait!" Thand interrupted. "Please, Princess, you don't owe us anything. You've helped us see our weakness and taught us to read and write. I don't want you to be put at risk again. I can seek out the wizard's help—alone, if necessary."

The king shook his head and sighed. "Thand, you are as foolish as my daughter to think this will be uncomplicated. Oden will lead a company of my best men to ask for Enunciation's help. I will allow you to join at your own risk."

"This curse must be undone. I'll take the risk, Your Majesty."

Then turning toward the princess, King Treutlen said, "Sharman, my instincts say that you must stay here, where you'll be safe."

"But, Father, you must let me go!"

"Be silent, girl!" her father snapped. "Must you always interrupt me?"

The princess fell silent but continued to meet her father's eyes.

Then, continuing in a milder voice, he said, "You are not invincible, although at your age it's common to think so. But you've proven that you are capable of surviving misfortune. Your friend, Thand, seems to share many of the same qualities. Therefore, I will I revise my order and allow both of you to make the journey with Oden. The Great Wizard Enunciation is a good friend and the only one I know who is capable of helping you resolve this problem. I will send a carrier pigeon ahead so he can prepare for your arrival. This conversation is ended."

The tension in the princess's body relaxed, and a slow smile replaced her frown.

"Thank you, Father. It is important that I do this," she said and embraced him.

Then Princess Sharman turned toward Thand and whispered in his ear, "Quickly, before he changes his mind."

They departed the chamber without seeing the smile on the king's face.

Chapter 14

*I*T WAS SPRINGTIME—A good time of the year for traveling. The rainy season was over, and a light breeze carried along the smell of new life. Preparations for their journey to Aerie Mountain had begun at dawn. The men worked vigorously throughout the day, and by mealtime they had stored the provisions, groomed their horses, and sharpened all their weapons. Not long after the evening meal, Oden ordered the company to their sleeping rolls so everyone would be well rested for the long journey. No cards or dice playing that night.

Against the queen's wishes, Princess Sharman slept near her traveling companions. She wanted to prove to the soldiers that no special treatment was needed. The princess also wanted to avoid a teary goodbye and a list of dos and don'ts from her mother, who was still angry with the king for allowing the princess to participate in this men-only journey.

The cock's crow announced daybreak. Sluggishly, the soldiers rubbed the sleep from their eyes, then gathered to share some warm porridge and hard biscuits. Afterward, they assembled in the paddock, making last-minute adjustments to their harnesses and saddles. Oden mounted first and the others followed his lead. He then circled the company, inspecting their equipment, assuring himself that the party was ready to ride. Satisfied, Oden gave the order to move out.

As they rode through the castle gate, a few well-wishers were on hand to offer them good luck and a safe return. The company passed through the adjacent village and into the fields. Even though the hour was early, men were already working the rich, black soil. Freshly planted fields spread west, while budding orchards covered the rolling hills to the east. There was little talk amongst the group, as thoughts of the task ahead overshadowed the morning ride.

The sun was approaching its midday arch when Thand noticed that the smell of horses had been replaced by the fragrance of wild flowers. All serious thoughts vanished as his eyes beheld a mead-owland of exploding color. Red poppies, white daisies, and yellow jonquils grew abundantly, with purple iris and bluebells mixed in as well. He had never seen a spectacle of plant life like this and couldn't imagine which words would best describe the scene.

Thand was considering staying in this field forever when Oden rode down the line and ordered the group to draw up.

"Rest your horses and let them graze. Then we'll continue through the daytime without interruption. You can eat as you ride. Once I find a suitable place, we'll stop to water the horses. Remember, darkness comes early in these hills. You've all been forewarned that the trail will become steeper and the ground less stable, so be careful."

Without waiting for a response, he galloped to the front of the column. In time, the trail began to move skyward. The meadow-land gave way to the forest, and the sun became filtered through a leafy canopy. The aroma of wild flowers was replaced with an earthy smell, heavy with pine. And the sounds of woodland creatures echoed through the trees.

The light turned softer as the travelers moved ahead. A faint moon appeared in the late-day sky, signaling that sunset was near. Another mile had passed when the sound of a stream cascading down the hillside alerted the horses to nearby water.

Oden moved off the trail toward the sound. The gurgling stream tumbled into a large pond made by some industrious beavers. The surrounding area seemed to be a perfect place to stop. Oden called out and motioned for the company to follow.

"We'll make camp here tonight," Oden said firmly. "You two men, get some firewood. You two, take care of the horses. Thand, you can unpack the saddlebags."

A fire was built for the princess, and a second was built for the soldiers, who camped closer to the trail.

Princess Sharman pointed to a spot close to her and said, "Thand, you sleep near me tonight. I may need you for protection."

Feeling like a warrior, Thand put his blanket next to the princess. But just as he began to get comfortable, the chilling sound of a lone wolf rolled through the campsite. Thand jumped up, all his senses on high alert.

"What was that?" he said, searching the dark woods.

"Don't you know the sound of wolves? They're dangerous animals—savage, my father said. But the fire should keep them away. Oden will post some guards just to be sure. Sit down," the princess said while tugging on his sleeve. "Maybe I need to protect *you* tonight."

Thand had heard the cry of a wolf before and this wasn't the same. He sat down with care and continued to scan the trees. Instinctively, he pulled his elbows close to his side, making himself as small as possible. The princess began talking about the day, but Thand was preoccupied with the night's sounds and wasn't listening. When the princess realized he wasn't paying attention, she shrugged, pulled a blanket around her shoulders, and blankly stared at the fire. A few yawns later, the princess curled up and drifted to sleep.

Thand's heart was racing too fast for sleep. He sat with his staff balanced across his knees and looked intently into the darkness, but the flames kept distracting him. Thand checked on Princess Sharman several times, but a soft snore told him she was deep in sleep. An hour into the watch, the hair on his neck stood on end when a new cry sounded. A high-pitched *Ahhh* followed by a deep *Hakk* emanated from deep inside an animal. *Ahhh-Hakk, Ahhh-Hakk.* The sound was answered by a second one—very close. Oden came rushing out of the dark, torch in hand, poking his flame at a snarl behind Thand's back. Bolting up, Thand turned and saw the wolf in a low stance, challenging Oden. Without thinking, Thand swung his staff but missed. The wolf lunged at him, biting into his arm just above the wrist. At the same time Oden shoved the burning torch into the animal's face. The wolf yelped, released Thand's arm, and disappeared whimpering into the darkness. Oden and Thand stood together, waiting for another attack, the smell of singed fur hanging in the air. Thand was shaking but stood his ground. Blood ran down his forearm and onto a small burn produced by the torch. At last, Oden lowered the flame, turned to Thand and inspected his arm.

"You're fortunate. That was an incurro-wolf, a very young incurro-wolf. A full-grown adult is the size of a pony and strong enough to snap the neck of a gray wolf. Think what it could do to you. This fledgling was still unsure of her strength."

Oden released Thand's arm. "Let the wound bleed a little. The wolf's spittle can cause infection. I have something in my bag that may help. And stay alert! If the rest of the pack is near, the horses could be in danger."

Oden returned and washed the wound with fresh water. Then Oden laid a peppermint leaf over the injury and wrapped it in a clean cloth.

"That should help for now, but hopefully the wizard will have a better remedy. You better add some more wood to the fire. It'll keep them at a safer distance. I'll add an extra guard to protect the horses."

All through the night Thand kept his fire bright. At one point a soldier brought him some more branches but told him to conserve. "You'll run out of wood at the rate you're burning."

About the time the stars began to dim, Thand's body relaxed and his chin dropped to his chest. When Oden shook him two hours later, Thand swore he had been awake all night.

The cool morning air mixed with the acrid smell of dying campfires. Princess Sharman sat up, stretched her arms above her head, and twisted side to side. "I slept like the ancients. How about you?"

Dark circles around Thand's eyes and black smudges on his forehead told the princess that he had experienced a different kind of night. "What happened to your hand? Let me see."

She reached for his hand, but he pulled back. "It's nothing."

Thand continued to roll his blanket. He didn't want the princess to know how foolish he had been the last night. *Why did I step ahead of Oden? Was I trying to be a hero, to show my bravery?* He stumbled over to get his plate of leftover beans and dry bread. Within the hour the company was back on the trail.

The princess had been silent all morning, waiting for Thand to explain the bandage on his arm. Finally, she let out an annoyed sigh. "Aren't you going to tell me about your hand?"

Thand's arm was throbbing, and he was in no mood for talk. "Talk to Oden. He'll explain."

The day continued sunny and dry, but the wind had been increasing as they moved higher up the mountain. A look over the side showed a drop that meant certain death. The column spiraled higher, and the pathway became steeper. Farther on, an old rockslide narrowed the trail, crowding them into single file.

By midafternoon, the pass had widened enough for the party to draw up. The air was thin at the higher altitude, and breathing had become more difficult. Oden gave an order to stop and rest the horses.

"Make sure you drink water and eat something. This is the only place on the trail wide enough for this purpose," Oden advised.

As they gathered to pass around a waterskin, a screeching sound was heard in the air. The men looked in the direction of the noise and saw a golden eagle screaming toward a soldier. The man dove for the ground as the bird veered off at the last second.

The bird of prey flew in a circle high above them, shrieking another warning. Then, at lightning speed, it lunged down, talons out front. This time the eagle didn't change course and raked the head of a packhorse with its sharp claws. The mare bucked and whinnied, moving dangerously close to the edge of the trail. Its kick loosened the gravel at the edge of the cliff, and the animal began to slide. A fast-thinking soldier jumped up and grabbed for the horse's reins, but it was useless. The beast and all the supplies plummeted over the side of the cliff. The soldier was horrified, but Oden ordered everyone to stand by the remaining horses and to use their staffs to ward off any new attacks.

As the angry bird screamed down again, Thand looked up at the higher side of the trail and saw a gnarled tree growing on the mountainside. A large nest was perched on top. Two eaglets could be seen looking over the side of the aerie, crying for their mother. Thand shouted to Oden and pointed toward the nest.

"It's the eagle's nest. She thinks we're a threat," Oden replied. "The mother is protecting her babies. Everyone, quick, let's move on. The bird should stop attacking once we're away from her chicks."

The golden eagle made several more dives, but the assaults were less aggressive as the travelers moved away from the nest. Keeping one eye on the sky, Oden sighed. "Looks like there'll be no rest today."

The shadows from the mountain were growing long as the group rounded a sharp curve. The treachery of the road had kept everyone focused on the ground. When Oden gave the order to halt, they stopped and looked up. Out of nowhere, it seemed, a dark fortress materialized. It appeared to be connected to the mountainside, like an appendage. Sitting on a chiseled-out plateau, the stronghold was built from the same gray-black stone as the mountain. The walls appeared like arms growing out of the dark cliff, hugging the castle, protecting it from harm. Towers, turrets, and chimney stacks rose above the battlement, overlooking a deep and darkening valley.

While the party waited, Oden rode ahead to the gatehouse. Twin square towers flanked the entranceway. It was not visible at first, but a deep chasm separated the road from the castle, giving the impression of a bottomless moat. A raised drawbridge prevented anyone from entering uninvited. On the wall above the barbican, a soldier stood guard.

Oden announced their presence: "Princess Sharman, daughter of King Treutlen, guardian of the realm, and her party are here to meet with the Great Wizard Enunciation."

Their arrival had been anticipated, so without acknowledging Oden, the guard barked an order to an unseen person. The grinding sound of rusty metal rattled behind the walls as a winch began to unwind. The infrequently used drawbridge creaked its way downward. The pulley screeched, and the first crack of light was seen in the dark wall. Oden had doubts that the mechanism would do its job, but the bridge-deck continued to lower. When the drawbridge was locked in place, a command was shouted for the party to come forward. The princess and her companions crossed over the chasm and under the sentry as they entered the castle.

Moving through the arched passageway, Thand was once again astonished by his surroundings. Inside the stronghold there was no visible greenery; everything was made of stone. Cobblestone filled the area where he expected to see grass. Large gray rocks were cut and perfectly fitted together to make the walls. Even the roofs were constructed with thin gray stone. The sounds of clogging hooves and jangling horse gear echoed throughout the enclave.

While the horses were tended to, the senior guard marched up, nodded to Oden, and bowed toward the princess. He requested they follow him to the palace entrance hall. Once within the doors, their eyes had to adjust to the poorly lit interior. Years of neglect had left the windows smudged; only shades of gray light were permitted to enter. Walking along the hallway, the fading light revealed dust motes floating in the air, while deeper inside, empty fireplaces allowed the castle walls to cast off its cold dampness. Wraithlike sounds echoed down the corridors, adding to the sense of gloom. Thand was thinking about retreating to the courtyard when suddenly, light spilled into the hallway as a door was thrown opened.

"There you are," said a cheerful voice. "Come in. Come in."

The voice belonged to the Great Wizard Enunciation. He was a thin man with long, white hair that trailed over his shoulders and a straggly, white beard that grew down to his chest. He had a long, knife-like nose, and bright, black eyes hidden behind thick, round glasses that gave his face the appearance of an owl. The wizard was wearing a deep-purple robe embroidered with ancient symbols. His skin was pale and translucent, as if a candle could shine through him. The wizard extended a bony hand from his dusty robe to greet his guests.

"Princess Sharman, look how much you've grown! The last time I saw you, you were being scrubbed by a nanny."

"I am sorry," she said, modestly crossing one arm over her chest. "I don't remember you, but Father has shared many wonderful stories about your intellect and powers."

"Yes. How is your father? We correspond through letters and messengers, but I haven't seen him in many years."

"He is well and sends his greetings along with a promise to see you sometime in the near future."

"He is a busy man with many responsibilities," the wizard said, nodding his wise head. "It would be nice to meet with him again."

A small amount of food and drink was brought to the wizard's private study. And stories, new and old, were shared. At one point the wizard asked about Thand's bandaged arm. Thand had been ignoring the injury, thinking he was stronger than the pain, but the heat on his arm and a throbbing headache said otherwise.

The princess pulled his arm toward the wizard. "Please look at it. He's pretending it's of no great concern, but Oden told me it was an incurro bite."

Enunciation removed the bandage and shook his head. A yellow fluid with a foul odor was draining from the wound.

"You're fortunate that you still have an arm. I have a remedy, if you'll allow me."

Without waiting for a response, Enunciation pushed on the edge of a wall panel. It spun 180 degrees, revealing a shelf. He removed some items and then returned. He opened a jar of white cream that smelled like sassafras root, applied it to the wound, and then wrapped it with a linen bandage. Thand's face winced from the pain, but he remained silent. The wizard raised the wounded arm above his shoulder and spoke.

"Trick of the trade, come to his aid.

Remove the bane that causes the pain.

Abolish the bite by the end of the night."

He told Thand to lower his arm and show him his hand. "Now, that burn is easy," he said and smeared the cream over the blister. As they watched, the swelling disappeared like a drop of water on a hot rock. All that remained was fresh pink skin.

The wizard let go of Thand's hand, and before they could comment on his magic, he said, "The day has been long, and it's time for you two to get some rest. I have some work that needs to be finished tonight if you want my assistance tomorrow. I'll meet you in the morning outside of my library. Good night."

Morning arrived faster than Thand thought possible. A small tray of fruit and cheese sat on a side table, but before he touched the food, Thand unraveled the yellow-stained bandage. His head jerked back in shock. He was repeating, "I can't believe it," for the third time when Princess Sharman showed up. Thand held up his arm for inspection. She squealed with delight. A two-inch patch of pale skin had replaced his festering wound. The tales of Enunciation's great power were true. His healing skills seemed beyond the normal boundaries of nature.

They walked a maze of dimly lit hallways, discussing the wizard's power and imagining what other talents he possessed. They rounded a corner. Thand stopped in mid-stride. In front of them was a bright and spacious passageway. Sunshine streamed in from tall windows on both sides, illuminating a beautiful, gothic, arched ceiling. They stepped onto the polished-stone floor and walked to a window. To the left, the mountaintops were smoky blue. On the right, in the near distance, a waterfall cascaded a thousand feet and then disappeared behind the landscape. It appeared they were standing on a bridge that linked the castle to another structure. An elaborately carved door at the end of the passageway opened suddenly, and Enunciation stood there as if he had materialized out of nowhere.

"Come in," he said with a playful look in his eyes. "Come in. I practically live in this tower. Occasionally, I have to sleep and eat. But as you may have noticed, I don't spend a lot of time in other parts of the castle—too much to do."

They stepped through the rune-covered door and into an immense room. The walls were lined with books, maps, and a sphere resting on a pedestal. The floor-to-ceiling windows allowed abundant sunlight to enter. Unlike other parts of the castle, housekeeping duties were carried out in here.

Thand pointed at the sphere and asked about its purpose.

"It's a celestial globe," Enunciation said. "I use it for charting the movement of the stars."

"I didn't know they moved."

"Yes. I'll have to give you a lesson sometime."

Thand looked up and spotted a second-floor gallery that was also stacked with books. A circular staircase spiraled to the upper floor, and a black cat, named Stygian, sat guarding the path to the top. Book-strewn desks and candles melted down to varying lengths revealed that the library was well used at night. The group walked toward the far end where the room angled to the right. Enunciation swept his arm and motioned for them to go forward.

Thand's eyes widened as he surveyed the area. The wall curved outward in a semicircle that was lined with tall, arched glass panels. Green marble columns supported a domed ceiling that was painted to look like the dawning day. On the east side of the ceiling, a curved panel of glass allowed the morning sun to shine through the dome. It was an ingenious design that gave the impression of an actual sunrise.

"This is my favorite room," the wizard said, as he seemed to grow taller with pride. "Designed to inspire new ideas. Walk over to the window, Thand. The mountain view is impressive."

Thand walked to the window's edge, looking out to where the peaks touched the sky. His eyes followed the slope of the mountain downward, and suddenly he felt wobbly. The room protruded from the castle's side, so nothing but emptiness was visible below his feet.

"Whoa!" Thand closed his eyes and backed away. "I felt like I was falling."

Enunciation laughed. Curiosity wouldn't let Princess Sharman stay in place; she had to walk to the edge and see for herself. She followed Thand's example, but when she looked down into the valley, she felt lightheaded and collapsed on the floor. Thand ran to her side.

"I'm all right," she said, sitting up. "I just needed to feel solid ground—quickly."

Thand helped her back to her feet then turned toward the wizard and said, "That's some effect you've created at that window."

"It's called vertigo, but that's not the effect I had in mind," the disappointed wizard confessed.

Enunciation pointed to one of several comfortable, high-back leather chairs and invited them to sit.

"Please take a seat. I promise the room is not going to fall into the valley. The idea is that this space is a launch point, a room where your imagination can soar beyond your earthbound thoughts. I can sit here all day, looking out, thinking of possibilities."

Enunciation sat in his own chair, then asked his guests to enlighten him on all that was happening at sea level, as he liked to call it. He was particularly interested in learning about the Elwins and the events on Lapis Lazuli Island.

Thand took the lead, with Princess Sharman adding to his account often. Their adventure unfolded gradually, and the wizard stopped the narrative many times to ask questions. He asked Thand to repeat certain pieces of the Black Storm so that he could better understand the cause and effect.

"That is quite a story, and magic is certainly at the root of the Elwins' problem," Enunciation observed. "I would bet that the fine dust was the agent for the spell, while the storm was meant to confuse and frighten. If we want to reverse the spell, the basic elements of reading must be incorporated into the enchantment."

The wizard pushed up his glasses. "Thand, what have you learned about reading?"

"I know that the alphabet is made of letters, and that the letters represent sounds. The order of letters and their sounds make words, and words are used to form sentences," Thand recited from memory.

"Exactly. And phrases are needed to make spells, along with a little sorcery. You see, wizardry without the correct words is like a lock without a key."

Enunciation got to his feet and swept his finger around the wall. "Searching through all of these books will be time-consuming, but it's the only way we'll find a solution to the Black Storm magic."

"All of these books?" Thand moaned. "It's impossible. I haven't a clue as to what I'm looking for."

"Look for anything that could be used to launch magic into the air or onto a person," Enunciation said, giving a supportive pat on the back. "You can start by searching in the books on that desk near the window."

Pointing to a tall bookcase attached to the wall, he looked at Princess Sharman. "These are my best references on the art of spell-breaking. You and I will begin there. Now, let's get started. No time to waste."

Thand collapsed into a chair and rubbed the back of his neck. The task seemed beyond the bounds of possibility, but he was determined to find a resolution and defeat Lord Creedy.

The fading light made reading difficult. Thand was rubbing his tired eyes when a short, plump man walked into the room carrying a flaming taper. He moved among the tables, lighting candles until the darkness faded away. Thand stood and stretched his stiff muscles. This assignment was like looking for a grain of salt in the ocean. He looked over at the wizard, whose owl-like eyes were following his finger across the page and down onto the next line. Princess Sharman's concentration seemed almost as intense. The passing of day seemed to have no effect on their resolve, so he sat back down and continued. Later on, when the wizard disappeared from the library, Thand turned toward the princess.

Stretching his back as he rolled his head, Thand said, "This is tiring. I didn't think sitting in a chair and reading all day would feel like work."

"It is work. You're using the muscle between your ears instead of the ones in your back."

Pushing his book away, Thand asked, "What are you talking about? I don't have a muscle between my ears."

"Lord Creedy would tell you there's only emptiness between your ears. But while your brain is not really a muscle, it works like one. The more you use it, the more you will accomplish."

"There are too many words I don't understand."

"Bring that large book over here and I'll show you how to use a dictionary."

It was late in the second full day when Thand pushed the books away. He closed his eyes and massaged his temples.

"Enough! How many more books do we have to read? We've been in here all day, and I can't remember a thing from this morning."

"Your brain is overloaded," said Enunciation. "Let's take a supper break."

They followed the wizard to a dark and gloomy dining room. In an earlier time, a warming fire and bright candles would have brightened the room. Two dozen people would have been sitting at the long banquet table, talking and laughing while servants bustled in and out, carrying trays loaded with venison, wild boar, and fish. An array of fresh vegetables and loaves of manchet bread would have also filled the table. Yet, on this evening, there were only three to share a simple meal in a drafty space with a dim candelabrum. They sat down to a bowl of pottage—a thick stew made of vegetables and meat. Ale and black bread rounded out the menu. Ironically, the food was served on fine porcelain dishes, but the contrast went unnoticed by Thand.

"Spices and vegetables are scarce in the mountains. I guess you can see from my weight that eating is a low priority." The wizard shrugged his bony shoulders as if to make his point. "Even though the food may not be tasty, I promise you, no one will starve."

Thand was skeptical.

After the meal ended, Princess Sharman and Thand decided to find Oden. The sound of laughter and bawdy language led them down a dimly lit hall. A turn to the left brought the twosome into a large, noisy room. The soldiers were in the far corner rolling dice—howling with excitement or shouting obscenities, depending on what number bounced from the cup. Oden was sitting alone near the doorway, watching the men and puffing on a pipe. The group playing games of chance paid no attention to the young couple as they entered, but Oden, who kept one eye on the door as a matter of habit, noticed them walk in. Leaving his pipe on the table, he stood to greet them.

"My lady," Oden said, with a respectful nod.

"Please, sit down, Oden. Don't let me stop you from your leisure."

Pulling two chairs over to his corner, he motioned for them to sit. The fireplace rendered the room bright and warm, a welcome change from the gloomy dining room.

Oden waited for the princess to sit. "How is your research going?"

The princess sighed and collapsed into her chair. "We haven't found a solution thus far, and it may be a long time before we see a bed. Is all well with you and your men?"

"Can't you see?" Oden chuckled. "They've been fed, and now they have their game. That's all they need."

Thand yawned. "It looks like it's going to be a long night of reading for us. By the way, have you seen the circular room in the library? It's like being on a cliff overlooking the valley, but you're protected from the wind and rain. You need to come back with us and see for yourself. There are enough books in that room to build a house. I saw a few regarding the sea. I'm sure you would find them interesting."

The princess knew that Oden's reading skills were poor, so she diverted the conversation and asked him about the history of the castle.

"There must be a reason why Enunciation lives in this empty castle. It's obvious to see that this was a grand place at one time."

"Yes, it was. And yes, there is a story that explains it."

The princess sat straight up in her chair. "Then I want to know the story."

After picking up his pipe and relighting the cold tobacco, Oden began: "The Duke of Glyndon was the previous owner. He was a wealthy man—but never satisfied. A number of years ago, he decided that he wanted greater power, and the mountain realm alone was too small for his ambitions. Ambition is fueled with money, so he demanded additional taxes from the Mystic Valley residents. Of course, they objected, but the duke threatened to burn their homes and confiscate their land if they didn't pay. Following a few nighttime fires, the townspeople recognized that they were no match for the mercenary soldiers. Enraged but unable to resist, they yielded to the duke.

"The story soon reached your father, and he was infuriated by the audacity of the duke. He had betrayed his responsibilities by placing his personal gain above the common good. King Treutlen could not let this insurrection go unpunished, so he assembled his military advisors to devise a plan to end the rebellion.

"The quickest route to Mystic Valley was over land, similar to the route we took. But the king knew the duke's army would be guarding the road. Your father was shrewd and decided to send his troops by ship instead of land. He selected the west side of Slate Mountain to stage the attack.

"The king had knowledge of a pass called Raven's View that cuts through Slate Mountain into the west valley. His plan was to divide the army into three companies. Two of the fighting units would land at Smuggler's Shore and work their way along the gap and over Slate Mountain. The third company, led by me, would stay on our ship and land near the northern end of Mystic Valley.

"On the morning of the attack, the Duke of Glyndon's army was camped exactly where your father had predicted. The king's army waited in the shadow of the mountain until the morning sun was in the face of the rebel army. The king personally led the flanking charge into Glyndon's army, whose soldiers were stunned and slow to react. The side attack drove a wedge, cutting the rebels in two. One of our regiments pushed the enemy toward Mystic Lake while the larger part drove in the opposite direction. This tactic forced the Duke of Glyndon and most of his army to retreat toward the open end of the valley.

"Dividing and conquering is a good strategy, but the king's

plan added another dimension. My army had closed off the northern end of the valley, and we pushed toward the center, thus forcing the enemy to fight on three fronts at the same time. By midafternoon most of the soldiers realized it was hopeless. Disregarding their leader's command, the soldiers chose to lay down their arms. By evening, the defeated Duke of Glyndon was found hiding in a cave. He was later returned to the capital for trial. The captured men were allowed to return to their families if they laid down their weapons and pledged fealty to the king."

"Lord Creedy would never have spared the soldiers," Thand said.

"This story is intriguing, but it doesn't explain how Enunciation acquired the castle," replied the princess.

"During the thirty-day war, Enunciation used his magical powers to heal the injured, but it came with a great cost to his own strength. Near the war's end, he was so frail that his own life seemed in jeopardy. King Treutlen saw the castle as a way to reward the wizard and allow him to regain his health. At first, Enunciation didn't want the castle because of its size and location; however, he had high regard for its library. When he discovered that the tower was above the normal cloud layer of the valley and that star-watching would be easier, he accepted the king's offer."

Just as the princess said, "That explains a lot," the short, plump assistant toddled into the room flapping his hands.

"Where have you been? Enunciation is questioning your whereabouts and wants to know how anyone can solve problems if they're playing with dice."

Thand exclaimed, "We're not playing dice! We're—"

Princess Sharman cleared her throat. "It's okay, Thand. Let's go."

Chapter 15

WHEN THAND AND Princess Sharman arrived at the library, Enunciation raised his head, grunted something incoherent, and then returned to his book. The evening break had refreshed Princess Sharman, and she was eager to resume her search. But Thand wasn't quite ready to start anew; being a scholar was much harder than he'd imagined. He moved aimlessly through the library, picking up books and then setting them back in place. Still unsure of what he was looking for, he walked up the spiral staircase and browsed through several more books. Stygian, the black cat, was keeping a watchful eye on him, as if she was sizing him up and deciding whether he would be allowed to remain in her domain. Thand must have passed the test because the cat tucked in her paws and closed her eyes.

After returning to the main floor, Thand still wasn't ready to pick up a book. Thand decided that observing Slate Mountain at night would be more interesting. Leaning forward, he cupped his hands around his face and stared out the window. The moon hung between the mountain peaks, casting a silvery light on the landscape below. Thand was searching for the pass through Raven's View when a dark shape flew across the moon. He pointed out the window. "I...I...think I just saw a dragon flying across the moon!"

Without bothering to look up from her reading, the princess said, "Don't be silly. There are no dragons in this world. You've worked your brain too hard, and it's playing tricks on you."

He had never actually seen a dragon, but in Elingale it was a time-honored fact that they existed. Thand turned sharply. "No, you're wrong. When I was younger, tales of dragons were retold often."

The princess forced a laugh. "That's ridiculous; I think I would know about dragons if they existed. My father would have told me, I'm sure."

"Your father didn't tell you about the war against the Duke of Glyndon. Maybe he wants to protect you from the scary things in life," Thand pointed out.

Her back stiffened. "I don't need protection from anything!"

"Not even Lord Creedy?"

The princess's posture slumped slightly. "Yes, I guess you're right. Maybe I've been shielded from some matters. But surely, if dragons exist, I would know about them."

Turning to face Enunciation, Thand asked, "What do you think about dragons? Do they really exist?"

Enunciation hesitated, then said, "Actually, there is a legend, but folklore is notorious for exaggeration."

"Tell me! Please."

A twinkle of mischief appeared in Enunciation's eyes. "Okay, but let's go into my favorite room so our imaginations can fly."

When the three were gathered around the light of a single candle, Enunciation took off his glasses and began.

"There was a small, rocky island with a jagged crag that jutted out of the sea. Day and night the waves battered the stony island, making it impossible to explore. High atop the buffeted cliff, a cave was carved into the stony side. At the mouth of the cavern, sitting on a bed of flaxen straw, was a golden egg about three feet across. The mythical egg was said to be that of a dragon and was visible from the shore. On a bright day, the sun reflected off the egg, casting out a radiant, golden light, beckoning to all who saw it. At night, a warm, orange glow pulsed from the embryo as if reflecting the life within the shell. Over the years, many people tried and many people perished trying to reach the dragon's golden egg.

"A young man, who lived near the cliff, was determined that someday he would make the golden egg his own. He searched for a year, looking for the perfect tree to chisel into a boat. Then one day, in a primeval forest that sits high above all others, the boy found what he was looking for—the trunk of a fallen ironwood tree. The name says it all, the wood was as hard as iron. And if he could chisel it properly, it would make a perfect canoe, capable of withstanding the battering waves. After weeks of exhausting work, he fashioned the ancient log into a seaworthy vessel. On a day when the murderous waves were more restrained than average, the young man paddled out to the rock. Fighting the deadly current with strength and determination, he reached the jagged rock and climbed out. At that moment, the waves reached up and pulled the boat under. If the boy tried to swim to shore, he would be smashed on the rocks. It was said that this was the sea's way of punishing the boy for daring to set foot on the island.

"Trapped on the barren island with no other choices, he continued his quest. Through persistent effort, he scaled the slippery cliff and reached the ledge close to the cave. Brushing the grit from his hands, he looked back toward the shore and saw a person standing at the edge. The young boy yelled and waved triumphantly. Turning back to the mouth of the cave, he looked at the golden egg. It was so beautiful, so radiant. The light reflected into his eyes, mesmerizing him. The boy shook his head to break the spell and carefully picked up the dragon's egg. The moment he touched the pulsating shell, he felt a burning desire to possess this treasure and never share it with anyone. Clutching his prized possession, the boy walked into the cave and was swallowed by the dark opening.

"Some said he nurtured the egg until the day it hatched. Then, as a reward, the grateful young dragon let the boy climb onto its back, and together they flew to a magical mountain where dragons reign. Others say the egg still lies deep in the cave, hidden from view, where the bones of the young man protect it from harm. Like most legends, the young boy was never seen again, and the location of the island has been lost in time."

Thand turned to Princess Sharman with a triumphant look, but she shrugged her shoulders and made no comment.

The wizard stood. "I have never actually seen a dragon. But the fact that the legends never die, and that new stories continue to be heard, makes me wonder if they may, in truth, really exist. Beyond that, I have no opinion. Now, go back to your reading. We've lost too much time already. We can discuss dragons at a later time."

The princess returned to her table and Thand, energized by the story, resumed his search.

For a time, the only sounds came from the turning of pages and the purring cat. Then Enunciation banged his fist on the table.

"That's what's missing!"

He made a quick notation, slammed his book closed, and quickly left the library.

"Did I do something wrong?" asked Thand.

"No, I don't think so," said the princess as she watched Enunciation leave the room. "Being alone all of the time can make people behave oddly."

Thand was bent over a book, head in hand, his mind numb. It had been over an hour since the wizard had disappeared.

Princess Sharman started waving her hands and shouted, "Thand! I think I've found it—a spell that will reverse the Black Storm's hocus-pocus. Let me read it one more time, and then we'll see if Enunciation agrees."

Thand got up, leaned over her shoulder, and asked, "What's hocus-pocus?"

"It's a word to describe magic."

"Then why didn't you just say magic? Why have two words that mean the same?"

"If you want to be a good reader, then you need to learn the meaning of as many words as possible. The collection of words you understand is called your vocabulary, and the larger your vocabulary, the better you'll be able to communicate with other people. And besides, isn't hocus-pocus a fun word to say?"

Thand was about to reply when Enunciation's assistant came into the room. "The Great Wizard Enunciation requests your presence. Please follow me."

A questioning look passed between them. Had Enunciation constructed his own remedy? The man led them along a well-worn passage and up a broad set of stairs. At the landing, the servant stopped and pointed to an opening that led upward. Without any further instruction, he disappeared down a dimly lit hallway, leaving them to wonder about his peculiar behavior.

They started up the tower cautiously. The stairs protruded from the outside walls and corkscrewed up the turret. Torch flames danced on the whistling wind while shadows bounced across the walls. There were no railings inside the poorly lit tower, and falling was a real possibility. As they ascended, the sounds grew more ghostly.

Words from a campfire story came to Thand's mind. *Flying shadows, souls of the dead, foreshadow evil ahead.* The words kept repeating in his head as he climbed higher. When they finally arrived at the top of the tower, Princess Sharman paused to catch her breath while Thand wiped the perspiration from his forehead.

"Are you okay?" the princess wheezed.

"That was easy," Thand said, gasping for air. "Let's go in."

They entered a large, circular room. Heavy wooden benches— cluttered with beakers, glass tubes, and jars of colored powders— filled the room. A glass globe, with no visible flame, hung from the ceiling, casting an intense light. Dried herbs and berries hung from the ceiling rafters, casting a sweet or pungent smell depending on where you stood.

Thand's eyes darted around the room, a thousand questions forming in his mind. He pointed to a large telescope aimed out a tall window. "What's that thing? Can you shoot birds with it?"

Enunciation had been mixing chemicals when they came into the room. "Slow down, Thand. I'll explain things as needed. That's a telescope, and it's used for looking at the stars and moon. It doesn't shoot anything."

"What's this yellow powder for?" Thand inquired as he picked up a jar.

"Leave that alone!" cried the wizard. "Put it down carefully. It makes things explode."

Thand's face turned white. He gripped the jar with both hands, warily set it back on the shelf, and stepped back. *I don't like the smell of it anyhow*, he thought.

He continued to explore, then halted when he saw a jar containing something suspended in a cloudy liquid. He whispered to the princess, "What's this?"

She looked at the thick mixture and cringed. "Animal parts. At least, I hope they're animal parts."

Princess Sharman walked toward the wizard. "I'm glad you called us up here. I think I may have found a method to dispel the Black Storm magic. In one of my books I discovered a spell called Erudite. It's supposed to unlock a part of the brain that controls reading and writing. The spell has a certain phrase that will disentangle the magic from the mind. It must be spoken very clearly, preferably from somewhere high. The phrase can only be spoken once; therefore, all involved must be present to hear the enchantment. A tower could be built so that the whole village could hear the phrase at the same time."

"That's not a practical solution," said Enunciation. "How can you build a tower without Lord Creedy's knowledge? Anyhow, it doesn't matter because I have my own solution. It won't work instantly, but in a short period of time the curse should go away. I don't need a tower or everyone to be present in order for this to work."

Princess Sharman mouth dropped open. "It doesn't matter? All of our hard work doesn't matter?" She turned her back, crossed her arms, and waited for a full explanation.

"Of course it matters. But my method has the best chance of succeeding. Lord Creedy won't see any suspicious activity. I'll use combination of special herbs, chemicals, and magic that can produce a corn plant with twenty-six rows of kernels in each ear. I have created a new spell to enchant the kernels with the sounds of the alphabet, and I'll use a second spell to make the plants grow quickly. The Elwins can plant the corn seeds, and within a week the stalks will be fully grown. Once the magic corn is harvested, the villagers will use it like any other grain. The effect will be similar to an antivenom serum that is used to heal snake-bites. The enchanted corn will enter their bodies and counteract the poisonous effects of the Black Storm spell. In a short amount of time, the Elwins will regain their reading skills."

He turned to Thand and asked if the village had a place where the corn could be planted and tended to separately. Thand nodded yes.

"Princess, if you could start mixing a few things for me. And Thand, if you could go down and have my assistant give you the seeds—he'll know the ones—then we can get started right away."

"But what about the Erudite spell? Are you just going to ignore my idea?" said the princess.

Hoping to appease her, the wizard said, "No, I'll add your key words to my enchantment as backup."

Thand saw the princess's back stiffen and knew she was not pleased. All of the time she had devoted to discovering an answer and Enunciation discarded her solution with hardly a thought.

As Thand closed the door behind him, the sounds of a disagreement arose. He proceeded down the stairs, shaking his head. Both proposals seemed to give the same results, but they each had flaws. The princess's idea was fast, but building a tower without it being discovered would be hard. The other was slow, and if Creedy discovered the corn before it was harvested, he would destroy it immediately. *Think! Is there anything I've read that could improve on their ideas?*

He stopped abruptly. The yellow powder in Enunciation's tower came to mind. He smiled knowingly, then quickened his step.

Thand burst through the library door and flew up the spiral

stairs to the second floor stack. The manual he was searching for had a section explaining the uses of the same yellow chemical that he'd seen in the wizard's laboratory.

I know the passage but which book? They all look the same. He was searching the first book when the cat meowed to get his attention. Stygian was sitting on top of a large book with one paw out and the other tucked underneath his shiny, black fur. The cat stopped licking his paw and looked at Thand with his emerald-green eyes that seemed to say, "Here it is. I've been waiting for you to return."

As he reached for the book, the black cat leaped to a nearby shelf. "Are you enchanted too? Or is this hocus-pocus?" Thand said as he grinned. Thand opened the book. *This is it!*

Thand returned to the lab and rushed through the door. His shoulders sagged—everyone was gone. He stood in the doorway, rocking in place while chewing on his bottom lip. *Where are they?*

He wandered through the lab, repeatedly looking at the door. *Have they gone to bed? The telescope—maybe I can find that dragon again.* He attempted to move the scope, but it was locked in place. Nevertheless, he looked through the lens and found an eyeful of stars. Uninterested, he looked around the room for another distraction. On the tabletop, by the window, he saw a large bowl with a mixture of powders and a mound of corn seeds lying next to it. *Where is Enunciation? Has he already finished?* Thand gave some thought to his next action. The Kookachoo Bird's words came to mind: "Open your mind, trust your instincts, and be prepared to take risks."

Thand walked past the table and over to the jar of yellow powder he had seen earlier. Remembering Enunciation's words, "It causes things to explode," Thand closed his eyes and took a deep breath, then carefully measured out what he believed was the proper portion. *I hope I understood that book correctly.*

He walked back to the bowl, poured the mustard-colored chemical into the mix, and then stirred. It didn't look any different. *Did I add too much or not enough?* He ran his hand through his hair. *What have I done?* His stomach felt queasy. *Why did I add anything at all?*

Thand stepped back and took a deep breath to calm his racing heart. *No, I must trust my judgment.* But his doubt refused to go away.

Time seemed to crawl as Thand continued to wait for Enunciation. He was beginning to think he'd have to spend the night in the lab, when the door swung open.

"There you are," the wizard said, annoyed. "Go downstairs and get some rest. I'll be up here the rest of the night and won't need any more help."

"But I have something to tell you. I think it's important."

"Not now! I have too much to do, and I don't need you distracting me with a lot of questions. The princess has already retired for the night."

Thand's body stiffened. "But this may help the spell work better."

The wizard waved a dismissive hand. "Go! I have it all worked out. I don't need any more ideas. Now leave, or I'll turn you into a bat!"

With that said, he pushed Thand out the door and slammed it shut.

Thand stood in the hallway and debated what to do. He turned back to the doorway and struck it with his fist several times. He waited. No response. He repeated the knock. Still the door didn't open. *Okay, ignore me. It's done and can't be changed. I'll have to take responsibility for my actions, right or wrong.*

Enunciation labored through the night. He took the words from Erudite, the princess's spell, and blended them with his own.

"Reading, knowledge...I hope I've calculated right. One spell is chancy, but adding a second is especially risky."

The black of night had faded to gray when the wizard finished his formulations and dusted the corn with his enhanced chemicals. He wiped his brow, and then, placing his hands above the concoction, he shut his eyes and recalled the language of the wizards.

"Alterations, germination, transmit the restoration.

Make it blossom; make it grow. Accelerate the maturation.

Complication, devastation, vanquishes the conjuration."

The wizard opened his eyes, clapped his hands together, and watched as the seeds shimmered briefly.

A smile crossed his face. "My most inventive creation to date—I hope."

A little after daybreak, Enunciation met his guests in the breakfast room and announced that all was completed.

"I'll bet my wizard's wand that this enchanted corn will reverse the Black Storm spell."

"If it doesn't," Thand said, "I'll send the dragon that I didn't see to pay you a visit."

"The princess said that, not me. I said—"

A shrill whistle stopped the conversation. Oden demanded everyone's full attention. Assignments were given to each person, and the remainder of the morning was devoted to preparing for the return trip.

By noon, the return party was assembled in the courtyard, and the magic seeds were placed in Oden's saddlebag. Enunciation gave the princess a hug and said, "There's enough daylight remaining to get past the most dangerous section of the trail before making camp tonight. I am sorry I can't go with you. I think my days of great adventures are over. I'll wait for your report telling me how well our magic formula worked."

Turning to Thand he said, "Learning to read has already changed your life. You are now a scientist and part-time wizard."

Everyone laughed but Thand. He was still worried that his scientific experiment may have unintended consequences.

Enunciation walked over to Oden, who was once again in charge of everyone's safety. "Oden, watch over the princess. I can see that she's not intimidated by danger—too much like her father."

By now, the sun had climbed above the mountaintops, and the afternoon promised to be fair and sunny. Oden took the lead and shouted a command, and the group filed out of the castle.

The mood was more relaxed as they proceeded along the trail. They knew the locations of the rockslides and the section where the path became dangerously narrow. When they reached the area where the horse had plummeted over the side, their defenses went on high alert. Oden scanned the sky, but the eagle that had threatened them earlier must have been instructing her young ones on the finer skills of flight—they were nowhere to be seen.

It was late afternoon on the second day of their journey when Oden brought his horse to a halt outside the walls of Adrianna Castle. Except for the eagle and the incurro-wolf attack, it had been an uneventful trip for him. But not so for Princess Sharman and Thand—they'd had a very successful meeting with the wizard. The seeds that were produced were somehow supposed to change life on Thand's island. Oden didn't entirely understand why all of this was so significant. Was reading that important?

The king was in the Great Hall, an audience chamber where the people came to ask for patronage. He had already settled a property-boundary conflict, appointed a new attendant for the queen, and approved a disputed guest list for a banquet to be held the next month. But still, a few more items were on the agenda.

King Treutlen yawned while two noisy administrators argued over some trivial rule. He pretended to listen but had heard the same petty squabble the prior day. His eyes had just closed when some excitement at the back of the hall drew his attention. The crowd parted and revealed Princess Sharman. The king's eyes grew bright as he rose from his throne.

"Precious Princess! Come here and tell me all that has happened on your journey. How is my old friend, Enunciation?"

The princess grabbed Thand's hand and pulled him forward. He let go to show independence, but his bravado was false. His previous exit from this hall was foremost on his mind. The princess wasn't offended and hurried toward her father. Thand pulled back his shoulders, looked straight ahead, and then walked down the runner like a toy soldier, arms stiffly at his side and knees barely bending.

No one seemed to take notice. Their eyes followed Princess Sharman.

"Now, tell me everything. I'm anxious to hear," said the king.

With her chin held high and beaming with pride, she related all that had happened. When the story was finished, she couldn't keep from saying, "I told you we could do it."

The king ignored the comment and turned to Thand. "I know you were successful, but did you have any additional encounters in the course of the trip?"

"Well, sir, I mean, Your Kingship, I survived an incurro-wolf attack, fought with an eagle, and saw a dragon fly across the moon."

"Yes," the king chuckled. "The high altitude can play tricks on the mind. Well, a carrier bird arrived with the news of your enchanted corn, and a ship is being prepared so that you may return to your island. I'm afraid Oden will have no rest from his duties."

"What about me, Father? I need to return to Lapis Lazuli and finish what I started."

The king put one hand on Thand's shoulder and held his daughter's hand with the other.

"You and Thand will be Oden's new lieutenants."

Chapter 16

*T*HAND STOOD AT the rail of Trident Seas, admiring Empeerean for the last time. The city seemed to drift away as the outgoing tide drew the ship back toward the open water. It had been three weeks since they'd set off on their journey, and while the days away had passed quickly, thoughts of the family, home-cooking, and his own bed made Thand eager to return to Elingale. He began humming the refrain from a sailor's song: "Leaving home, only to roam, makes the heart grow fonder, to return from the yonder."

Orders were shouted and sails began to drop as the heavy boat made the turn toward the sea. Thand was worried that the boat sat lower in the water than he recalled. But a sailor told him it was due to the additional weight of soldiers and horses and that he shouldn't fear since the weighted boat was more stable. Even with the sailor's reassurance, he still couldn't dispel the vision of a large wave swallowing the low-riding ship.

Thand spent most of the day on deck. Oden was right, the ship had become a second home. That night he jumped into his hammock with a new appreciation for comfort. Gone was the hard, rocky ground, replaced by the gentle rocking motion of the ship.

The morning air was motionless when he stepped outside.

Streaks of red and black covered the sky and reflected seamlessly on the flat sea. The crimson light rebounded upon the sails, creating an impression that they had been soaked in wine.

Thand voiced wonder. "I can't believe the sky! The whole world seems to glow red. It's beautiful."

Brevis, standing nearby, gave a sideways glance. "Then you mustn't know the old proverb: 'Red skies at night, sailor's delight. Red skies in morn', sailors be warned.' Be watchful today."

Before noon, the skies darkened with menacing clouds, the wind began to strengthen, and the sea transformed from smooth and green to choppy and gray. Rumblings of thunder were heard to the east, and the ship began to roll. The bow plunged deep into the waves, and seawater swept over the deck. Soon, angry whitecaps encircled the ship like an invading army.

Oden warned Princess Sharman to stay in her cabin and then went searching for Thand. Bouncing from one side to the next, he stumbled to the main deck and tracked down Thand.

"You should return to your cabin. We're in for a blow."

Thand's eyebrows drew together in a questioning manner.

"A storm, lots of wind, huge waves—could be dangerous," Oden clarified.

The ship seemed to give life to Oden's words as it pointed upward and then quickly pitched down into the water. A booming reverberation was followed by cold water foaming around their ankles. Oden looked over and saw Thand's face turning pale.

"I don't have time to take you below deck, and it's gotten too rough for you to make it back alone. Stand in the middle, under the main mast. The ship rolls the least at that spot. And hold on tight as you move about. In this sea there's no way to be rescued. If you go overboard, you're as good as dead."

Thand swallowed hard. Oden's warning clung to him like salt

to the sea. He picked his way across the deck and was nearly run over by a rolling cask. Stumbling uphill, then quickly downhill, while being pushed side to side, he scrabbled toward the center. Now he understood why crabs needed so many legs. When he finally reached the mast, he hugged it like a little boy holding unto his mother, then wished to be back in his village where the only thing that rolled was the hillside.

Waves continued to grow higher, and the ship pitched so far to the side that Thand was sure it was going to roll over. His grip was growing weak when he found a length of rope and tied himself to the mast. At times he saw nothing but the iron-gray sea, while other times he could only make out lightning exploding across the sky. The bow buried itself in monstrous upsurge. A sailor flashed by—reaching, grabbing for anything close at hand—but the huge wave washed across the deck and he was gone. Every muscle in Thand ached from the strain of holding on to the mast. His lips and chin were trembling from fear and cold, while the rain continued to lash at his face for over an hour. At length the rain came to an end, and the merciless wind began to subside. The storm that had seemed eternal had moved on, but the gray-green sea remained agitated late into the evening.

Three days was the normal sailing time between the islands, but the storm had added one more. And so Thand was overjoyed to hear, "Land-ho, Lapis Lazuli Island," shouted from the look-out's nest.

The moon was hidden behind thick clouds, making it virtually impossible for the ship to be seen from land, but that advantage would be lost if the moon returned. No one on the island, especially not Lord Creedy, could know of their arrival. So, exercising a great deal of caution, the captain dropped the anchor early.

Oden looked out toward a dark profile that represented the island. They'd have well over a mile to cross tonight. The overcast sky showed no sign of breaking before dawn, and only a faint breeze blew across the flat sea. Now was the right time to go ashore. The longboat was made ready, and the bag of enchanted seeds was handed to Thand. Worried that they might fall overboard, he placed the precious kernels between his feet. His restless legs bounced up and down while he anxiously chewed on his bottom lip, worrying that Lord Creedy might discover them.

At first the rowing was easy, but a shift in the wind altered that. Sore muscles, strained backs, and blistered hands continued to plague them as they rowed against the breeze. Oden had brought along a chalk stone and told the men to rub their hands with it. The powdery white stone would improve their grip and help reduce blisters.

An hour of steady pulling landed the party on shore. Oden used silent hand gestures to secure the boat and then prompted Thand to lead the party. With slow, cautious movements, Thand moved toward the village using an indirect route.

There were only a few houses with light coming from their windows, but one of them was Thand's. He saw a shadow pass in front of the window. *Probably Eschon,* he thought. A smile came to his face as he tiptoed to the back of the house, imagining the look on his brother's face.

Thand rapped lightly on the door and then walked in. Eschon jumped up in surprise.

"You're home! It's about time," Eschon said in a sharp tone. "Where have you been?"

Thand stopped in his tracks and stared at his brother in disbelief. Eschon's eyes appeared dead.

"When's the last time you ate or slept?"

Eschon gave a dismissive laugh. "Why do you care?"

Thand looked around the room and knew something was wrong. His mother would never have allowed the house to look this unkempt.

"What's wrong? Where's Mother?"

"She's in a dungeon! She's been there since you sailed off and left us to deal with Lord Creedy on our own."

"Calm down, Eschon. Why are you acting like this? You think we've been on a lark since I left? The three of us were in danger more times than I wish to remember. I didn't expect a hero's welcome, but I didn't expect to be condemned for trying to help Elingale. Now, sit back down. Tell us what's happened."

Eschon looked down at his feet and wiped a tear from his eye.

"I'm sorry, Thand. I've been scared and unable to do anything since Creedy took Mother. He sent a bunch of men to the house, and I couldn't stop them. All I know is Creedy won't let her out of his prison until she tells him how the princess escaped and what we plan next. As far as I know, Mother hasn't said a word."

"It's my fault!" said the princess, reaching out for Eschon's hand. "If I hadn't interfered with your life, none of this would have happened."

Eschon avoided her hand and said, "That may be true, but then we'd still be treated like we were Creedy's personal property."

Then Thand pointed his finger directly at his brother. "And you know I left here because we decided that our lives needed to change. Have you forgotten everything? Aren't we trying to transform our present way of life into something better?"

"Let's all calm down," Oden said in a level-headed voice,

pushing his palms toward the ground. "Eschon, tell us what happened since we left the island. Then Thand will tell you our plan."

Eschon pounded his fist against his knee and jumped up. "The only plan I want to know about is the plan to get my mother home."

Oden didn't flinch. "That will happen very soon. Part of our strategy is to arrest Lord Creedy, and then your mother will be released. You can go with the soldiers yourself and open the cell door."

"Great! Let's go now."

"Eschon," Thand said, looking hard into his eyes. "Be reasonable. If Creedy suspects anything, the first person who will suffer is Mother. Please calm down."

The confrontational mood slowly changed over the next hour as Eschon learned about the trip to Aerie Mountain. Eventually, Oden stood, stretched, and then suggested it was past time that everyone got some rest. Daybreak was not far off.

Princess Sharman climbed the ladder and was surprised that she'd missed the loft. Oden found a corner where he could curl up. And the brothers went to their room—but not to sleep. Eschon had settled down and now wanted to know every detail of what Thand had experienced since leaving home.

The splendor of the palace, the reclusive wizard named Enunciation, his castle in the mountains, and the sea-sickening trip back to the island were all described in detail. Eventually, the black sky began turning gray, but Thand had saved his best stories for last. He moved close to Eschon's ear and whispered, "We must try to rest, even if it's for an hour, but there are two things I want to tell you that no one else knows. I added something to the enchanted seeds, and I saw a dragon."

"A dragon," Eschon squealed loudly. "Really?"

"Be quiet! No one believes me, but I knew you would. Now, we must sleep."

"Sleep! How can I sleep after you've told me that? Was it breathing fire?"

Just after sunrise, the two brothers decided it was time to inform the villagers of Thand's return and give them details of what to expect in the coming days. When Thand walked out the door his face went slack. The noxious smell of rotting garbage and spoiled vegetables filled the air. His mother's and all of Elingale's cherished gardens were choked with weeds, and when he looked to the right he saw the charred remains of Treelore's house. An unexpected desire for revenge filled Thand. His face stretched into a snarl.

"What's happened?" It was a statement more than a question.

Eschon's hands clenched repeatedly. "Lord Creedy was furious when he discovered that Princess Sharman had escaped. He sent his thugs to intimidate us, but that didn't work. So he took Mother as a hostage and then forced us to work from sunup to sundown. The fire happened when we were in the field. No one knows how it started, but we have our suspicions."

Thand's mood darkened further. His desire to extract punishment for a wrong had never been stronger.

"What's wrong? I've never seen you this angry."

"I'm disgusted that we've let ourselves sink to this level. Our ancestors lived here before the Creedys, but we've let them take hold of our land and our lives for an unfulfilled promise. The Elwins have always sidestepped conflict, and look at the results.

Yes, I'm angry, but mostly with myself for never defying him before now."

Thand swallowed hard and then strode toward the fields with a new sense of determination.

During the daylight hours, Princess Sharman and Oden stayed busy dividing the sack of seeds into small packets. At one point Oden paused and looked at the princess, scratching his jaw.

"When I first met them they were anxious and fearful. Now, I see determined and unafraid. How'd you do it?"

"I used reading to open the door to other possibilities. I showed them how education can transform their lives. Once the Elwins began to understand the benefits, they headed for the door. When Lord Creedy tried to slam it closed, they revolted."

Oden looked down, reluctant to look at her directly. "You know my reading skills aren't so good. I've spent all my time learning to read charts, not books. Am I too old to be taught writing?"

Princess Sharman rushed to him like she had on the day she was released from Creedy's prison.

"Never!"

It was dusk when the boys returned from the field with the good news that the planting was finished and that there had been no sign of Creedy's people. Now it was time for Princess Sharman and Oden to return to the ship before they were discovered. A decision was made for Eschon to stay behind and watch for any unusual activity.

At the rear of the house, Thand steered them toward a deer trail where the trees quickly closed around them. They had covered half the distance to the beach when Princess Sharman stepped into an unseen rabbit hole and wrenched her ankle. Oden examined her foot by carefully stretching it in all directions. The pain was considerable but not sharp. He determined that the ankle wasn't broken, but badly sprained. A crutch would be needed. Thand searched the underbrush and quickly found a sturdy tree branch. He snapped off pieces until the branch resembled the letter Y. The prop was a little too short, but she tried to make it work. They started forward again, but the princess was still having trouble walking. She put her arm around Thand's shoulder for added support. He was more than happy to oblige, but the sound from the two of them hobbling through the woods—crunching leaves and snapping twigs—made concealment doubtful. The thinning brushwood and rising moon helped to advance their progress. The edge of the forest was in sight when Princess Sharman stopped abruptly and raised her hand to point.

"Look," she whispered. "Something's out there."

A flash of light reflected off of a steel blade.

"Got you now!" a big man said as he jumped in their path, waving a wicked-looking hunting knife that was normally used for skinning animals. "Won't Lord Creedy be glad to see you? Len, tie their hands."

A second person stepped out of the dark.

Thand tapped the hand of Princess Sharman as a signal to let go of the stick.

"Run!" Thand shouted as he swung the crutch at the head of the knife-wielding man. Oden charged the second man.

Thand's blow hit the target, but it didn't stop the man from swinging the knife at Princess Sharman. She tried to dodge the blade but wasn't quick enough, and a red line appeared across her upper arm. The princess screamed and Thand swung once more.

Oden charged his man and struck him low with his right shoulder. The air rushed out of the man's lungs when he slammed into the ground. Oden jumped on top and pinned one hand to the ground, but the attacker had found a palm-sized rock and hit Oden in the side of his face. The assailant rose to his knees, ready to strike again.

Thand smashed his club into the attacker's knife-hand. The stick broke on impact, but it still knocked the knife from his hand. When the bandit bent down to retrieve the weapon, Thand joined both of his hands together, forming a V, and bashed him on the head. The man went down, but he was not ready to give up. The attacker groped for the blade, and Thand pinned his arm with his foot; but the man reached back with his other arm and knocked Thand off his feet. The attacker had the size and weight advantage and easily rolled on top, pinning Thand with his knees. The big man reached for the weapon, and then a scream echoed through the woods. A sailor had crunched the assailant's hand with a hard stomp of his boot. Thand twisted away and picked up the knife.

"Halt!" said a voice, as a second sailor appeared behind Oden. The attacker swung his stone-fisted hand at the knee of the soldier, but the soldier was ready and hit the man with the butt of his rifle. Stunned, the man fell face-forward to the ground, with blood running down the side of his neck.

"Good work!" said Oden, jumping to his feet. "I was beginning to wonder if you had fallen asleep or returned to the ship without us."

"I'm sorry I didn't spot them sooner," said one of the sentries. "They're most likely trackers because they were as quiet as deer."

Oden looked down on the two men. "Who's in charge?"

The scrawny man pointed to the large one. "Shepherd is."

"Keep your mouth shut, Len."

"I told you, Shepherd, this was a bad idea. These Elwins are much smarter than Creedy thinks."

The guards stood the bandits on their feet and pushed them toward the beach.

Thand brushed the sticks and leaves off his clothes and looked for the princess. She was leaning against a tree at the edge of the sand, pressing her hand around the knife-cut in an attempt to stop the bleeding.

"Let me see that," Thand said.

He ripped the bloodstained sleeve from her shirt and soaked it in the salt water. "I need to clean the wound."

Thand washed the cut with salt water, while the princess's face wrinkled from the sting. Then he packed some wet seaweed over the wound and bound it on her arm with the torn sleeve. He took her hand and smiled. "You'll be okay."

She looked at the bandage suspiciously. "Are you positive it won't get infected? It looks like a bush is growing out of my arm."

"It'll work—that is, if your *Methods of Healing* book is correct."

"You better have read it correctly," she snapped.

"I did. Why are you so hostile?"

"How would you feel if you had a twisted ankle and a stab wound?"

"Not good, but I'd be grateful if someone had just put himself or herself in danger to help me."

She started to say more but stopped and stared at the ground for a quiet moment. Her eyes softened, then she looked up with a mischievous smile. "Come here, so I can show you my gratefulness."

As Thand stepped forward, a guard's voice shattered the moment. "What should we do with these two? Ahem, I mean the prisoners."

Oden's eyes flared with hatred as he grabbed Shepherd's collar. "Use one of Creedy's techniques to make them talk."

The sailor applied pressure to the big man's smashed hand, and the man became quite cooperative. He informed them that they'd been hunting nearby when they heard the heavy sounds, discovered the princess, and saw a way to redeem themselves. Lord Creedy had blamed his tracking party for letting her get away. If they could capture her, and then return her to Lord Creedy, he would forgive them and perhaps even reward the two with some gold.

"What now?" asked the soldier.

"Well, I can't let them go," said Oden. "They'll run back and tell Creedy we're here. Put them in the boat and tie them together, back to back."

"But you can't do that," protested Len. "What if the boat overturns?"

"Then you'll have company on the bottom of the sea."

Thand nudged Princess Sharman and they stepped to the water's edge. Moonlight silhouetted Trident Seas, and the only sound they heard was from the waves washing onshore.

Staring at the ship, Thand cleared his throat. "Is this where we say goodbye?"

The princess stepped closer to Thand. "No, not goodbye, just see you tomorrow."

"I didn't think the captain would allow you to return until Creedy was under arrest—too dangerous."

"He won't be happy, but I made it clear before we set sail that there would be no restrictions on me. You and I have come this far together, and nobody's going to stop us from finishing."

Thand's body relaxed. "Good. Then I'll see you when the enchanted corn is ready?"

"Maybe sooner, if I can convince Oden."

"Thand," Oden said as he stepped out of the shadows, startling them. "I'll meet you on the beach each morning. You can let me know if Creedy is causing any problems and also let me know about the corn's progress."

Thand was beginning to believe that all of these interruptions were intentional. "I will."

"And don't forget, the cavalry is ready when needed. The captain is moving the ship closer to the island."

Then Oden looked at the princess. "The prisoners are in the boat. It's time to go."

Thand's shoulders slumped as he realized that his moment alone with the princess was gone. He watched the sailors shove the boat back into the sea, and then, after a weak wave, he turned for home.

Chapter 17

DARK CLOUDS, A rumble of thunder, and suddenly panic gripped Elingale.

"Lord Creedy," someone whispered anxiously as he looked at the sky.

"Another storm to destroy our magic corn," moaned another.

But their fear was short-lived. Unlike the Black Storm, this downpour was a gentle, soaking rain that lasted less than ten minutes. The rainfall appeared to have been a part of Enunciation's strategy because within an hour the corn began to grow. At first, tiny white shoots pushed the soil aside, and then rows of pale green plants began to sprout. By late afternoon, the stalks were nearly a foot tall. The workers couldn't believe their eyes. A week's worth of growth had occurred in a single day. The Elwins wanted to dance or hug each other, but they had been warned about public displays of enthusiasm. If Lord Creedy learned of this, the magic corn would be ripped out of the ground and destroyed instantly.

The following day two absent-minded boys were working in the field, scaring birds from the crops, and they started talking about the new cornfield. One insisted it was magic corn while the other said it was a new type that grew fast. Both were right, but the quarrel was overheard by a Creedy worker, who dropped his rake and ran to the mansion to report what he had heard.

Lord Creedy's face tightened as he listened to the news. "Child's talk," he said to the worker and then flapped a hand to send him away. The door closed, and he began to pace the floor. He made an effort to convince himself that there was nothing the Elwins could do without his knowledge. However, the day before, the workers had seemed more restless than normal. Maybe he was overthinking this problem, but he had to be sure.

The following day Creedy sent a worker to carefully inspect the field near the village and report back. The man returned to a reception area in the mansion and waited. An hour later, Lord Creedy sauntered into the room carrying a jug of water. The worker looked at his selfish boss, then dabbed the sweat from his own brow.

"I'm waiting," Creedy said as he took a drink.

The parched man wiped more sweat from his brow, related what he had overheard, then described seeing the stalks wriggle out of the ground like green smoke.

Lord Creedy turned his back on the worker and glared in the direction of Elingale. *Not possible, unless magic is involved— and if that's true then this isn't about growing more food.* He set the water on a table and picked up his cane. After several circles around the room, he swore under his breath and slammed the cane on a table.

He turned and harshly pumped his index finger into the man's chest. "Start looking for strangers. Someone is helping these villagers, and I want to know who. NOW!"

As the frightened man ran out the door, Lord Creedy's thoughts turn to Baylock—*he's capable of making this happen.*

Lord Creedy had slept badly, worrying about this new problem. He couldn't figure out any practical connection between the quick-corn and the Elwins. What would they gain by growing this plant? How and when they had gotten it was just as disturbing. However, if magic was being used on his island, Baylock would have to be involved. The wizard's reputation and independence had grown over time—an irritating fact that bothered Creedy greatly. However, if he wanted answers, he had no other choice. Throwing his hands in the air in frustration, he called for his carriage.

Creedy was restless and agitated when he arrived at Baylock's home. The trip north had seemed longer than normal, and he was certain that the coachman had deliberately driven at a slow pace.

He's part of this conspiracy too, Creedy thought. *Everyone's working against me. That'll change soon.*

Creedy jumped out of the carriage and slammed the door. He scowled at the driver and said he'd deal with him later. Next, he marched to the front door and barged in without waiting. He paraded past several empty rooms, then saw a dim light at the end of a hall. Following it to a small, windowless room, he found Baylock bent over a table, cutting on a slimy object. Creedy stood in the doorway, tapping his foot compulsively while he waited to be acknowledged. The wizard ignored him, so he cleared his throat and began tapping his serpent cane on the floor.

"Lord and master, I am glad you've returned," Baylock said sarcastically, without looking up. He continued to dissect some small creature that was resting in a shallow pan.

"I have a new pet project, and it will need funding. I hope you've come to purchase more of my services."

"Shut up, you fool, and listen to me. I've found an unusual field of corn growing in Elingale. The stalks are rising at least a foot every day. It has to be enchanted, so I know you're involved. Explain yourself!"

Baylock seemed pleased to know something was irritating Creedy. He shrugged his shoulders and smiled.

"I've never heard of magic corn, except in a fairy tale. It seems that you have yourself a new problem."

Creedy made a quick, disgusted snort. "Who's paying you? I demand to know!"

Baylock looked Creedy directly in the eyes. "I don't have any involvement, but I wish I did. And you don't demand anything from me. I'm not your servant. Solve your own problem!"

Lord Creedy brooded a moment before he conceded that he couldn't do this without the wizard. He wouldn't look Baylock in the eyes and nearly choked on his words, but he asked for help.

The wizard put his hand to his lips to hide a smirk. Creedy asking for his services—he'd finally brought the mighty land-lord to his knees. Against his better judgment, he decided not to humiliate Creedy any further; after all, he needed money to fund his demon project.

"Is there any sign of that girl from Adrianna Island? She seems to have a strong attachment to the Elwins. Maybe the princess has returned to settle the score with you."

"What does she know about magic? If she could use it, she would've escaped my prison without the help of those fools."

"It may be *who* she knows, not *what* she knows that's important.

Creedy's left eyebrow lifted. "That means that the princess would have to know someone like you."

"Yes, but unfortunately it wasn't me, and I don't allow competition on my island."

"Your island?"

"Sorry, I must have been thinking ahead."

"Why does she care for those simpleminded Elwins? They can't give her anything she doesn't already have."

"There are other motivations besides power and greed."

"I'm not familiar with any of those. Nevertheless, I am ready if she does come back. I have my spies searching for strangers, and if I find any…let's just say I won't be so kind."

Baylock laughed. "*Kind,* now there's a word I don't associate with you."

"Do you want to banter words or make money?"

Baylock didn't answer the obvious question but put his work down, washed his hands in a dry sand mixture, and then headed to his library. An hour had passed slowly when Creedy turned to see the wizard coming up the hallway with a downcast expression and rubbing the back of his neck.

"I am not sure what's causing that corn to grow so rapidly. I don't know of any spells that are able to perform what you describe, and—"

"You're a worthless, no-good conjurer, Baylock. You're telling me that the Elwins have a better magician than you."

"Shut up! Unlike you, I can work through a problem without running to someone else to solve my troubles. Follow me if you want a solution. Otherwise, get out."

Lord Creedy's body tensed like a person preparing for a fight, but his rarely-used common sense intruded as he realized that alienating Baylock wouldn't help solve anything. He watched the wizard walk toward the library, hesitated a moment, then hurried to catch up.

Baylock led the landowner downstairs into a warm, airless cellar that looked more like a small cave. Creedy followed but was suspicious of the wizard's intentions and shifted his serpent cane to his right hand—ready to strike. They walked past bubbling beakers and jars of colored powder. In a far corner, there was a wooden table with leather straps and cutting instruments hanging directly above. Creedy's eyes darted around as he tried to determine the purpose of this bizarre room. Distracted, Creedy bumped into Baylock when he stopped in front of a locked metal door.

"Pay attention," Baylock scolded. "And be careful. There's danger on the other side of this door."

"This better be good. I've never heard of a spell locked behind a door."

"No spell, but the perfect solution, my friend. Fire! It solves so many problems. When in doubt, burn it out," he said, laughing.

Baylock unlocked the airtight door, and a hot, putrid smell flooded the room. Creedy coughed and gagged.

"What in damnation is that smell!?" he choked out, pinching his nose and waving a hand in front of his face.

Baylock laughed. "The smell of success."

Inside the room, hanging upside down from the ceiling, were hideous, bat-like creatures. They were black as the night, hairy, and larger than any normal species known to Creedy. These beasts had large nostrils, small red eyes, and yellow teeth shaped like daggers.

"My flying friends here are called bohes," said Baylock. "They have a wingspan of five feet and can snort a flame as hot as the sun. They have a screech that will drive a person to madness. Best of all, the bohes have never failed to do my bidding. When they're finished, nothing will grow in that field—at least not in your lifetime."

Creedy looked a little closer and noticed that the creatures had serpentine necks and small, pointed tails. "Those things look like they were created by the Prince of Darkness. I have no doubt that they're capable of burning a field or anything else," Creedy said as he coughed. "Let's get out of here. I feel like I am in the waiting room of the devil."

"You will be, one day," Baylock mumbled under his breath.

They withdrew from the cellar and went upstairs for some fresh air. After the two hammered out the details of their plan, Lord Creedy headed back to his estate, his worries and his wallet lightened.

Chapter 18

*L*ORD CREEDY CLIMBED onto his favorite horse, a chestnut-colored mare named Russet. He leaned forward and patted her on the neck. "From this day forward we will celebrate this moment, old girl. They will never defy me again."

He galloped to a hilltop overlooking Elingale and scanned the normally pristine village. A rare smile formed on his face.

"Look at that village," he said to his disinterested horse. "Crumbling mortar, roofs that need thatching, and garbage that's piling up—the long hours in the fields are really showing. The village-mother remains silent, and now they've come up with a new scheme to defy me. My patience has ended. After my new flying friends destroy their magic field and Grace pays a visit to Mactabilis, they will never defy me again."

Creedy glanced over his shoulder to the east and laughed. He stood up in his stirrups for a better view and watched the dark cloud approach. "Now they'll learn."

It was just before noon when a villager pointed to a dark spot in the sky. At first it looked similar to black smoke, but the quickly changing shape suggested something else—maybe crows. As the black form advanced, the Elwins realized that the size of these mysterious birds was immense. There was no cawing or other sound except the rhythmic whooshing of their massive wings. As they passed overhead, the downdraft of wind was enough to stir the hair on the Elwins' heads. Scores of villagers began to tremble; others started running. The beasts were black with red eyes, and their bodies were malformed. Their tails were round, like a rat, but then forked at the end, like a snake's tongue. Their wings were bony and leathery, consistent with a bat's, but that was their only similarity to the bats that darted in the evening sky. These creatures were too large, too quiet, and their necks were elongated, comparable to a duck's.

The fiends flew silently overhead, as if they were on a mission, ignoring the villagers below. The silence was suddenly shattered when the hideous monsters reached the magic corn. An earsplitting cry followed by a shockwave of heat stunned the nearby Elwins. Liquid fire spewed from the mouths of these black villains as chaos gripped Elingale. Some people fell to the ground and covered their heads; others froze in place, too shocked to move. The furnace-like roar smothered the shouts of, "Run for cover," and, "Run for your lives." People collided with others as the villagers crisscrossed the field like scattering ants. Many ran for their homes and others ran under trees, trying to shield themselves from the flying monsters. There was horror in the sky, terror on the field, and utter confusion everywhere.

The screeching bohes continued to stream across the fields while jets of fire exploded from their nostrils. In seconds, the green stalks began to smolder. The smoke and fire mingled in the air, creating a sharp, peppery smell that irritated the eyes and skin. Soon, a sizzling sound was heard, and then the magic kernels began to explode. The bursting noise was strange—not a popping sound as might be expected, but the actual sounds of letters from the alphabet.

"It sounds like the field is chattering," said one Elwin to another as they hid underneath a tree.

Thand's mind was racing, searching for answers, while the gibberish sounds filled the sky. The babble evoked a memory, something that was said in Enunciation's library; then it all made sense. The kernels' popping noises were the sounds of the alphabet. The alphabet is made of letters that represent sounds; the sounds make words, and, as soon as Thand remembered that words make spells— boom! "Reading is the key to knowledge" thundered across the sky. He knew those words. They constituted the essential phrase used in the Erudite spell—the spell Princess Sharman had discovered.

The words seemed to flutter in the air for a moment, like butterflies. Then, as if a huge tree had suddenly split open, a loud cracking sound split the air and a jagged bolt of lightning forked horizontally across the cloudless sky. A deep, long roll of thunder followed. Then, just for a second, all motion ceased, and complete silence reigned. And then, the chaotic sounds of panic returned. Some raced to stomp out the crackling fire while others ran to the grotto for water buckets, hoping to save their thatched roofs.

Thand grabbed his brother's hands and started to spin him in a circle like the children's game, crying, "We did it. We did it!"

"Did what?" asked Eschon as he whirled around, questioning Thand's sanity.

"Don't you see? This should release us from the spell."

Eschon stopped spinning and looked sadly at the smoldering field. "But we haven't used any of the corn, and it doesn't look like we ever will."

Thand pushed his brother forward. "Quick, let's go to the house and check my theory."

Lord Creedy was filled with enormous satisfaction as fire poured from the sky and smoke began to rise, but then a peculiar noise made his smile turn to confusion. The sound of corn popping—that was odd…it seemed like speech. His heart rate increased, and then—boom, "Reading is the key to knowledge" exploded in the air.

Gripping the sides of his head, his body began to shake. "No! No! This can't be true." Then the sound of his cry was replaced by an animalistic growl. He kicked Russet in the flanks, yanked hard on her reins, and galloped back toward his estate. A plan for retribution was already forming in his mind.

Thand and Eschon dashed through the smoke on the way to their cottage. Bursting through the front door, the boys ran to a stack of papers sitting on the desk. Thand picked up the top page and thrust it in front of Eschon.

"Here, try to read this."

Eschon read the words out loud: "'If you can read these words, the spell is broken.' Yes, yes, I can read it! It's signed 'Princess Sharman.'"

Thand grabbed the paper, unable to stand still, and ran outside. They stopped each person they saw and asked him or her to look at the paper. Every last one was able to read the page. They ran to the edge of the then-simmering cornfield, and to the boys' surprise, there stood Princess Sharman and Oden.

"What are you doing here?" Thand asked, breathing heavily. "I thought you were staying on Trident Seas until I set the signal fire."

"I know. That was the plan," Princess Sharman agreed. "But we were talking over our strategy while the captain brought the ship closer to the island, and then we heard a horrible screeching sound coming from an enormous flock of black birds. What were those things?"

"We don't know, but they breathe fire and made that awful noise you heard," Eschon said, rushing his words.

The princess's confusion increased as she surveyed the ruined field. "But what was the popping sound? We thought it might be gunfire and were afraid that Creedy had attacked the village. Then I was stunned to hear the words from the Erudite spell blast over the treetops. How did that happen? What caused the corn to explode? Has Creedy beaten us again? Everything looks ruined. Did all of our work go up in smoke? Is the spell broken?"

Thand put up his hands. "Whoa, slow down! I can't answer all these questions at once. To answer the last question first, yes, it looks like the spell has been reversed. We found the piece of paper you left in the house, and everyone who has looked at it can read your words."

"Great!" squealed the princess, doing a jig and clapping her hands. "Do you know how the words to the spell got spoken?"

Thand looked down at his feet. "Well, I added some powder to Enunciation's creation. Do you remember the yellow powder that was in his lab?"

"Yes, I remember. He was quite angry with you when you picked it up."

"It turned out to be useful. When the wizard told me that the powder could explode, I remembered something I had read earlier in the day. I went back to the library and searched for a manual. Somehow, Stygian, the black cat, was sitting on top of the book I was looking for. I know I had put that book back on the shelf, but anyway, I opened it to the description of the yellow chemical."

"What did you find?" she asked impatiently.

"I went up to Enunciation's lab, but he wasn't there. I waited for a long time, and when no one showed up, I decided to add the chemical. Later, the wizard came rushing in and shoved me out the door before I could explain what I had done. The next time I saw him, the corn was enchanted. I was afraid to mention the addition because nothing could be changed. After those creatures set it on fire, the yellow powder caused the corn to explode. The explosion of the letters formed the words to your spell, and that's why it was heard by everyone."

"But how did you know there was going to be a fire?" asked Eschon.

"I didn't. I thought that the heat from the sun might cause the chemical to work. I was wrong, but the flames from those big bats, or whatever they are, made it happen."

Not caring what people thought, Princess Sharman grabbed Thand and gave him a kiss, then did the same to Eschon.

"You did it! We did it! Enunciation's enchantment, your exploding chemical, and my Erudite spell all combined to reverse the spell. It hardly seems possible."

Eschon, still smiling from the kiss of a princess, quipped, "That's why they call it magic. Right, kin?"

"Good job everyone," said Oden warmly, as he patted each one on the back. "Looks like you outsmarted Lord Creedy."

Eschon's smile disappeared. "Not yet. He still has my mother."

"She hasn't been forgotten. As soon as I get the men and horses unloaded, Creedy will pay for his deeds."

Eschon gave a crisp nod and the foursome started back home. Soon, they came to the village crossroad. One path led to the beach, and the other curved back to the village. Eschon looked at his brother and tactfully said, "You two to go to the beach and get the fishing net. I think it needs repair. I'll see you back at the house in a little while."

Oden exchanged a collaborative smile with Eschon. "I'll go with you. Someone in the village may need medical attention."

Chapter 19

As soon as Creedy arrived in the mansion, he went straight to his writing desk and pulled out paper and a pen. He dipped his quill into the inkpot and began a letter to Baylock. His anger increased with each pen stroke. When Lord Creedy was finished, he stamped the ink-splattered letter with his seal and placed it in a messenger pouch.

Creedy marched to the stables, mumbling to himself and kicking anything that was in his way. "I'll teach those Elwins that I'm the master of this island. They're going to pay dearly for challenging me."

By the time he reached the barn, he was shaking uncontrollably. *Where is everyone?*

Unfortunately for Myke, Creedy's mumbling wasn't heard in the stable. Lord Creedy kicked open the door and scanned the area. Myke ducked into a horse stall, but it was too late.

"Come here, you coward. Deliver this report to Wizard Baylock. He must have it before nightfall. And ride like your life depended on it—because it does."

Frightened, the stable boy took the pouch and ran to Alacrity, his favorite horse. Ignoring his normal preparation, Myke threw a saddle on her back, cinched the strap, and climbed on. He leaned over and whispered an apology for not brushing her first. Then, with a gentle nudge to her flanks, he skillfully guided the horse out of the barn.

Just past the fence gate, Myke spurred Alacrity to gallop, hoping to impress Lord Creedy with his sincerity. A half-mile down the lane, Myke gave a quick look back to make sure they were out of Creedy's sight. He gave a slight pull on the reins and brought the horse to a canter. A few hundred yards farther, he stopped completely.

The road forked just around the bend. One trail led north to Baylock, and the other path tracked to the beach where the Elwins fished. He shifted in his saddle to look back at the mansion, then turned around and looked at the split. He tapped the pouch and chewed on his lip while struggling with his choices. His eyes darted back and forth as he murmured to himself, "Creedy or Elwins. Elwins or Creedy." One meant food; the other meant nothing. Then he sat straight up in the saddle, shoulders back, chin up, and urged Alacrity to run.

Eschon walked across the beach with a whimsical smile on his face. Of late, his brother seemed to get distracted easily around Princess Sharman. Why else would he have forgotten to bring the fishing net home yesterday? When he stooped to pick up his torn net, he saw someone riding toward him. He straightened up just as Myke pulled on the reins and sprang off his horse.

Eschon's eyes narrowed. "Aren't you the stable boy who works for Creedy? What are you doing here?"

"I think Lord Creedy is planning something terrible. He was in an awful mood when he handed me this message. I'm supposed to deliver it to Wizard Baylock, but I think you should see it first."

Eschon took the pouch and pulled out the dispatch. It was time to test his reading ability. He read the note slowly, then read it again. Crumpling the letter in one hand, he looked into Myke's eyes. "You're right. This is awful. We must find Princess Sharman right away."

Myke climbed back on Alacrity, then reached his hand down to Eschon. "Climb on; I'll take you anywhere you need to go."

It was midafternoon before the field fires had been completely extinguished. Most of the villagers were gathered in the common square, trading stories. A few were just learning that they could read again. The crowd hushed when they saw the boys gallop into the square.

Eschon pointed out Princess Sharman, and Myke guided Alacrity toward her. Eschon pushed himself off the back of the horse before it came to a complete stop and ran to the princess, handing her Creedy's message.

"You need to read this right away. It's from Creedy. Does this say what I think it does?"

He walked a tight circle, chewing on his lip, while she read the letter.

"This is terrible! Creedy is ordering Baylock to release his creatures—on Elingale!"

The Elwins' faces turned white when they heard the words.

"Our village will be burned to the ground!" cried Eschon. "I don't understand."

"You have paid no heed to his rules and have outsmarted him

too many times. His rage has turned him into a lunatic," said Oden. "He doesn't see that he'll destroy himself by destroying you."

Eschon grabbed Thand's forearm. "Mother! We must rescue her right now."

Trying not to imagine what would happen to her, everyone turned to Oden.

"You're right. We don't have much time. I'll send a man to the ship right now, but it will be dawn before they're all assembled and ready for fighting."

Eschon stared incredulously at Oden. "Dawn?"

"I think there's enough time. Thanks to Myke's bravery, Baylock doesn't know Creedy's plan. And Creedy's not expecting to see Myke back at the mansion before tomorrow. Have the villagers start gathering bandages and ointments."

"I knew it," Myke said to Eschon as they walked to the house. "Every time Lord Creedy went to see Baylock, something terrible happened afterward. I'm sure the wizard must have created those monstrous bohes."

Eschon tilted his head to one side. "What's a bohe?"

"That's what Creedy called the bat-creatures. He said they were bats out of hell."

Myke was added to their inner circle and asked to gather with them inside the boys' house.

"Before we do anything else, we rescue my mother," insisted Eschon. "And I'm not going to stay behind this time."

"But we also need to deal with the wizard. He's the destructive force in all of Creedy's schemes. If we don't stop Baylock right away, he'll take over where Creedy left off."

"Why don't we split up and capture them at the same time," suggested Thand.

"That's possible. I'll send the cavalry to arrest Baylock."

Eschon stood. "I want to be with the group that attacks Creedy. I want to see the fear on his face when he realizes that he has lost."

"Eschon, I can't let you get in the way of the soldiers. It's too dangerous," said Oden.

"I won't interfere. I just want to be the one who unlocks the door for my mother."

"Then I'll be happy to give you that honor."

"And I have a better idea than just marching up the main road. There's a hidden path to the mansion. It'll be much easier to surprise Lord Creedy if we use it," Eschon said.

Oden smiled. "Now you're thinking like a soldier."

Eschon looked at Myke with a hopeful expectation. "You know the quickest way to Baylock's house. Will you help us?"

Myke's eyes widened as he looked around the room. "I've had my wages taken away and been to the punishment room too many times. I'll do anything you need."

Thand scrutinized Myke for a moment. "You've proven yourself to be a friend of the Elwins. Welcome to the family."

Chapter 20

THE DECKHAND LOOKED over the side, poised to throw the sounding line. He remembered, six feet to a fathom. When ordered, the weighted-line plunged to the bottom. "Ten fathoms by the mark," he called and hauled the line in, only to drop it once more. "Nine fathoms by the deep, sir."

Captain Boreas was trying to avoid running aground in the dark while shortening the distance to land. He was taking the chance so that the horses could swim the length and still be strong enough to ride once onshore. At three fathoms, he ordered the anchor dropped. Now it was up to the military men.

Soldiers had been lined up for almost an hour, waiting for the order to disembark. When the command was given, they climbed into the boats and were ferried to the shore. A defensive perimeter was formed around the shoreline while several scouts were positioned farther inland. Next, saddles, bridles, weapons, and supplies were loaded on longboats and brought to shore. Finally, the cavalry horses were fitted into a unique hoist and lowered into the water. Instinctively, the horses swam to shore, where they were gathered and then herded into a makeshift corral.

Several hours before sunrise, all the men, armor, and animals were ready for duty. A heavy mist had formed in the last hour before dawn, allowing the army to enter the village unseen. Only the jangle of horse tackle had revealed their movements.

A strategy had been prepared during the night, and everyone was eager to begin the mission. Myke and the cavalry sergeant would lead the horsemen north to Baylock's, with Princess Sharman and Thand following. Eschon and Oden would lead their men on foot to Lord Creedy's mansion.

On command, the cavalry galloped out of Elingale and headed to the alpine region of the north. It became obvious in the first mile of travel that Thand was not proficient at high-speed riding. Princess Sharman offered a few balancing tips, and told him to relax his grip on the reins.

"It's similar to getting your sea legs. You need to move with the motion of the horse."

Thand attempted to do as told, but he bounced more than floated with the horse. It was a long, uncomfortable ride, but despite some saddle sores, he managed to arrive within a few minutes of everyone else.

The first sergeant had his men surrounding the house when the two stragglers rode up. Thand painstakingly dismounted and waddled over to the sergeant, who was trying to suppress a smile. Myke stayed with the horses to guard against a rear attack.

Cautiously, they went to the front door and pushed on the latch. To everyone's surprise, the door was unlocked.

"Wait," the sergeant whispered. "Too easy."

They stepped back while a soldier used his musket to nudge the door. A metallic click sounded, then a flash of light and smoke erupted. Everyone dove to the ground but the disciplined soldiers kept their rifles trained on the door. Nothing but silence followed. A moment later, a hand signal from the officer brought the soldiers forward. It'd been a delaying tactic, the sergeant decided, and then he led his men up the stairs.

Princess Sharman and Thand began to investigate the main floor. Within a few minutes, they discovered the door to the wizard's library and snuck in. This library was not as extensive as Enunciation's, but still, hundreds of volumes lined the walls from floor to ceiling. On the right side, several rows of bookshelves extended from the wall, creating bays. At the front end of one extension was a wedge-shaped marble rock with an ornate rapier thrust into its center.

"What's that?" the princess said, pointing to the mysterious block.

Thand walked over to examine. "It looks like someone stabbed the stone with a sword, but that would be impossible."

He grabbed the sword and tried to free it, but it wouldn't budge. Atop the sword's pommel was a blue sapphire button. A curious push triggered a nearby section of the floor to soundlessly drop and slide. A shadowy cloud of rancid air moved upward from the black hole.

Princess Sharman turned her head and closed her eyes. "Whew, it smells like something died down there."

Thand fanned the air in front of his nose. "It reminds me of the stench in the field after the fire. Someone went to a lot of trouble to hide that entrance. There must be a reason. I've got to find out why. You wait up here."

Princess Sharman glanced at the floor opening. Creedy's dungeon was still fresh in her memory and climbing down into a dark place didn't appeal to her at all.

She swallowed hard. "You don't go anyplace without me. Don't even try."

"Okay," Thand nodded, a little too fast.

Looking around the library, Thand spotted a rack of torches hanging on the wall. A flint and steel kit sat on a nearby table. Princess Sharman picked up the kit and walked toward Thand. He held the torch, and she began to strike the steel against the stone. After a few hits, a spark ignited the torch, and they moved toward the trapdoor, black smoke trailing. With one hand clutching the flaming light and the other holding the princess's hand, Thand slowly led her down the stairs and into the unknown.

The ladder-like steps creaked with the weight of each footstep. Cobwebs dangled in their faces. When they reached the last step, Thand swung the torch in an arc. The area had a low, vaulted ceiling made of ancient brick. Heavy tables, glass beakers, and jars of powder were reminiscent of Enunciation's lab. The odor was nauseating. Off to one side was a large metal door built into a rocky wall. Thand crossed the room to investigate and discovered the entry was locked. He started patting his clothes, looking for something—anything—to pick the lock. He felt a long slender object, pulled it out of his pocket, and held it up to the light.

The princess's eyes widened. "The key to my chest. I wondered where it was."

"Eschon found it in the dirt after you were kidnapped. You must have lost it when struggling with Creedy's men. I've been meaning to give it back to you, but we've been so busy I forgot."

Thand put the key in the lock and turned it, but nothing happened. He cursed and tried once more but got the same result. The princess asked Thand to step aside. She pulled out the key and held it close to her face.

"Don't fail me now," she whispered, then rubbed the key between her hands and reinserted it. She jiggled it and then gave it a twist. The tumbler moved inside, and with a click, the door opened.

"How'd you do that?"

"Magic," she said with an impish grin. "Hocus-pocus."

Thand scratched his jaw. "That key is a mystery. Someday you'll have to tell me its history."

The stench doubled when the door swung open. They flapped their hands in front of their faces, trying to make the putrid smell go away, but the effort was wasted. They covered their mouths and noses with their forearms, glanced around uneasily, and then cautiously stepped through the door. Thand held the torch above his head and examined the place carefully. He spotted dark droppings on the floor, but otherwise, the room seemed empty. Carefully, he walked toward the back and discovered that it continued into a tunnel. Princess Sharman, never more than a few inches behind, encouraged him to go on. A short distance down the tunnel, she stumbled. Her hands went to her mouth and she moaned—something fleshy was at her feet. Backing away with a shudder, she questioned her decision to come. Thand spun around, and the torchlight reflected off a rotting bohe lying on the floor. Princess Sharman turned away and gagged.

Thand reached out to steady her. "Must be where the bohes lived."

"No wonder everyone was so frightened when they saw those things. I hope there are no more here."

The princess stepped around the large, bat-like creature and continued. The tunnel took a sharp turn to the left and brightened. At the far end of the passage, light was seeping from the edges of a door. As they forged ahead, the air became cooler and the terrible smell grew fainter. No side trails where found, and when they arrived at the end, muted sounds of crashing waves were heard coming from beyond the door.

Princess Sharman tilted her head, questioning.

Thand put a hand on the door. "Let's find out."

The door was heavy. Thand had to make use of his shoulder, but the door opened with a groan. Blinding light flooded the tunnel. For a moment all they could see were white spots in front of their eyes, but the smell of the sea and the sounds of crying gulls alerted them to the location. Shading their eyes, they stepped out onto a wooden wharf that was anchored to the base of a steep cliff. Gazing out to the sea, they saw whitecaps and diving seabirds. Several hundred feet ahead stood a rocky outcrop jutting from the sea. The formation acted like a reef and calmed the water surrounding the dock. It was the perfect place for a small harbor. But despite the safe haven, there were no boats to be seen.

"Dead end," said Thand.

"Great escape tunnel," observed the princess.

The two filled their lungs with fresh air and turned around. Retracing their path and carefully avoiding the dead bohe, they returned to the library, where the first sergeant was trying to pull the sword from the stone.

The red-faced sergeant cleared his throat and asked Thand for a report.

"There's a tunnel in the cave below. It runs beneath the house and ends up at the bottom of a cliff. Baylock must have had a boat tied to the dock and used it to leave the island."

Suddenly the color in Thand's face drained. "The bohes! Where did they go?"

Chapter 21

*E*SCHON WATCHED THE last man ride out of Elingale heading north. He had been waiting for this moment since Creedy's thugs took his mother and humiliated him. Now it was time for retribution, time to make Creedy experience the type of punishment that he inflicted on everyone else.

A final equipment check was made. The captain nodded and Oden signaled Eschon to lead the way. Eschon expelled the pent-up air in his lungs. Never could he have imagined a moment like this. He strode forward with long steps and chin held high.

The army filed out of the valley and past the burnt cornfield, where the pungent smell of sulfur still remained in the air. In less than a mile, Elingale faded behind the hills, and a deep ravine appeared. Eschon pointed to a neglected path that disappeared into a tangle of brush and motioned for the men to follow him.

A battle for sunlight was being fought by the vegetation at the forest edge. Low hanging branches and prickly thorn bushes crowded each other, making entrance into the woods difficult. Once the soldiers fought through the scrappy bushes, the fight for daylight moved to the treetops. The remaining plant life had survived by adapting to life with a diminished amount of sunlight.

The area beyond the thicket opened into a high, open canopy

and conveyed a sense of peaceful solitude, but the struggle forward wasn't over. Interlacing roots rose up to trip anyone who wasn't careful, while the early morning mist contributed to missteps.

"This ravine will keep us hidden from Lord Creedy's sight," Eschon promised.

"How did you know about this trail? It's perfect for avoiding detection."

"We Elwins have spies of our own. This is how we can secretly watch Creedy if needed. But the path will only get us to within fifty yards of his house. Then you'll have to use the main road."

"That's close enough to take him by surprise," Oden said.

For the next half-mile, they moved quietly along the wooded trail. A rapid *pik-pik-pik* echoed from a distant woodpecker, while nearby frogs croaked a greeting. At one point, the pathway descended, then disappeared under a wide stream, reappearing on the far side. A few well-placed stepping-stones made the crossing easier. The ravine rose, then flattened at the edge of the trees. The road leading to Creedy's mansion lay just beyond.

Eschon held up a hand. "This is as far as we can go unseen."

Oden went down on one knee. He looked closely at the mansion, then back down the road.

"Eschon, I want you to stay here. You're not trained for this, and I don't want you to get hurt."

"But you said I could rescue my mother."

"No, I said you could unlock the cell door. There's no way I can let you into the house before I have Lord Creedy under my control."

Oden searched for a safe spot.

"There," he said pointing to a broad oak tree. "Climb into the branches and be my lookout. If Creedy catches sight of us too soon, he may run. You'd be in a great spot to let us know in which direction he escaped."

Eschon stalked away, then turned back. "You want me to hide in a tree? How does that help rescue my mother?"

"Believe me, a lookout is a very important job. You're the eyes of our army. Without someone to watch the area, we could walk into a trap."

"I don't know . . ."

"Look, Eschon, we may have to use these guns. I don't want you running around and getting shot. Please, be my lookout. It's important."

Eschon took a deep breath and exhaled slowly. *Getting shot isn't going to help out Mother . . . and maybe it's an important job.*

"I'll agree if you promise not to let anyone else open the cell door before I get there."

Oden nodded agreement.

"Okay," Eschon said as he looked up at the sturdy oak limb. "I should be able to watch from up there and still be unseen. Just make sure someone is close enough to hear me."

Oden divided his men into three squads.

"Remember, no noise, and only use your weapons as a last resource. Let's go."

Four soldiers swept right and five went left toward the barn. Oden took the remaining three and converged on the main entry.

The men rushed forward, and before Lord Creedy could realize that the stable boy hadn't returned from Baylock's, the king's soldiers kicked open the door and started to search. Lord Creedy was in his bedroom, just finishing fastening his shirt, when he heard thumping boots downstairs and headed toward the noise. Oden was just starting up the steps when he spotted the lord coming down the hallway.

"What's the meaning of this?" yelled Creedy from the top of the steps. "Leave this house at once!"

"You're under arrest for the kidnappings of Grace and Princess Sharman—and numerous other crimes against the Elwins," Oden announced.

Lord Creedy looked past him to see several soldiers blocking his escape. He stopped and smoothed down his clothes, displaying confidence.

"I don't know what you're talking about. But give me a moment, and I'll come downstairs to discuss this accusation."

Then he turned and sprinted down the hall to his bedroom, where he propped a chair under the door handle, jamming it closed. He rushed to the dressing room, opened his wardrobe, and pushed the clothes to one side. He stepped in and closed the door, locking it from the inside. The key rotation triggered a four-foot square panel in the back wall to glide open; a button on the other side made the opening disappear.

"Figure that out," he taunted as he squeezed through the opening.

His escape route led down a hidden staircase and into a tunnel that emerged through a trapdoor in the equipment shed. Creedy pushed up, peaked around, scrambled out, and dashed inside the barn. He was so winded by now that running was out of the question. The barebacked Russet was close at hand. But Creedy hadn't saddled his own horse in years, and he was accustomed to having help climbing on the horse. Out of options, he turned a bucket upside down and clumsily climbed onto Russet's back. Then, pulling on the reins, he turned for the barn door just as five soldiers stepped in the doorway and pointed their muskets at him.

"Halt!" they ordered.

Lord Creedy looked to the other stable door. It was still clear. He pulled hard, turning his reluctant horse. Then bending low, he galloped toward the opening. Rifles flashed, gunpowder exploded, a bee-like sound whirred past his head, and wood chips flew. He cleared the door and looked back to see gray smoke filling the barn. "I never lose," he said, laughing.

Standing on a large branch above the lane, Eschon heard the gunshots and looked down the road to see Lord Creedy charging toward him.

His heart raced. He was the only one standing between the landlord and his escape. His knees trembled. What should he do? Only one thought came to his mind. He bent his knees; his timing had to be perfect. The landlord was almost under him; he jumped—a second too early. Eschon landed between the neck of the horse and the front of Creedy. The forward momentum knocked them both off the back of the horse. Creedy hit the ground hard, and Eschon heard a sharp crack as he landed on top of him.

Creedy had acted like a cushion and softened Eschon's fall, but he still had forward momentum and bounced into a tree, striking his head. Eschon lay dazed, unsure of his surroundings, and then the sound of Creedy crying in pain brought him back to the moment. He raised himself into a sitting position and reached for his head. Blood was flowing from a gash in his forehead, and a knot was forming quickly. The landlord was about five feet away, rolling from side to side, blubbering that his leg was broken. Eschon looked over and realized what he had done, then whooped loudly.

"I did it! I stopped Creedy."

Eschon tested his own legs and was able to stand, though he was still wobbly. He leaned against the tree and regained his awareness, then walked casually over to Lord Creedy, crossed his arms, and looked down. He fought an urge to stomp on Creedy's injured leg and make him feel some of the pain he had inflicted on others—that kind of pain was only short-term. Creedy needed to suffer the misery of imprisonment: where he took orders instead of giving them, where he begged for decent food and clean water, and where the luxuries of his great house didn't exist. That's the kind of pain he deserved.

Oden ran up and examined Eschon. His shirt was bloody, his hands were scraped raw, and the bump on his head continued to grow.

Oden wrinkled his brow. "You look pretty beat-up. Can you walk?"

Eschon thrust his chest out and looked back at Creedy. "Never been better."

Then Eschon turned to Oden. "So much for the safety of the trees."

"You're a hero!" Oden shouted. "You vanquished the invincible Lord Creedy."

The soldiers encircled the moaning Creedy and then stood him up. With no allowance made for his comfort or pain, Creedy was thrown across a horse's back and tied. Maxim Creedy screamed threats at the men, but no one listened—his power was gone. The mighty man had been reduced to common baggage.

Eschon wanted to stay and take pleasure in the moment, but he had something of greater importance to deal with.

Eschon ran into the room, clasping his left hand to his chest. Breathlessly, he asked, "Has she been released? Does she know I'm here?"

The waiting guard smiled at Eschon and presented him the key.

Eschon rushed down the steps to the iron door, stopped, brushed himself off, and then inserted the key. He opened the rusty door, expecting his mother to leap out and hug him, but instead he saw a drawn-up woman, huddled in the corner, sitting on a pile of filthy straw. She hadn't even turned toward the sound of the creaking door.

He let out a sharp gasp and then moved closer. "Mother. It's me, Eschon."

Grace turned toward the voice. She blinked twice while searching for recognition. After a moment of uncertainty, her sagging face began to tighten, and then it brightened into a radiant smile.

"Eschon," she whispered, and she tried to stand.

He ran to her, raised her up, and then squeezed her tight. Her color was dull, and the weight loss was noticeable. Her hair had thinned, and he could feel her ribs.

Eschon wouldn't let go as he rocked her side to side and spoke softly into her ear. "What has that monster done to you?"

With an unsteady voice she answered, "Nothing. They gave me food, but I couldn't eat. I was too worried about you boys."

"We're fine," he said as he took a step but still held on to her shoulders. "Thand is home and soldiers are bringing Lord Creedy here right now. His days of causing suffering are over."

Chapter 22

*I*T HAD BEEN quite an exciting day. Creedy was in prison, Grace was safely at home, and no one had been seriously injured. The word spread: Lord Creedy was behind bars and powerless to strike back. The filthy chamber that he had forced Grace and Princess Sharman to live in was now his home. With a joyous shout, the workers threw down their tools and headed for home.

The villagers began drifting into the town square to talk over recent events. Living without Lord Creedy was the main topic. All hoped that the most noticeable change would be a reasonable workday. Although Creedy's harassments would end, no one was sure how his foremen would react. Would they try to take over his properties and continue to overwork the Elwins, or would they become more sensible? One thing was certain, no one in Elingale understood how to operate a business. This topic was too serious for their mood, so the conversation shifted to Princess Sharman landing on their shore. No one could agree if it was destiny or chance, but all agreed that it was the most significant event of their lives.

Someone suggested that they become less serious and add more cheerfulness to the evening. Patwick and his son agreed and gathered some logs to start a bonfire. At the same time the fire was being fueled, benches and tables were carried into the square. And before long, a barrel of ale was rolled out. Sensing a party, Eschon ran back into the house and returned with armfuls of food. Someone went to get a couple of fowls they said needed roasting; another had a pig. A pit was dug and filled with hickory wood. Before long, the meats were dripping sizzling-fat into the fire; the smoke added a delicious aroma to the night air.

As the evening continued, Thand's neighbor dusted off his mandolin and began to pick a tune. Within moments, a fiddler appeared, and then another. Once the music started, dancing was not far behind. Children grabbed hands, circled the musicians, and sang to the lively music. Eschon was in a jovial mood—tonight would be a celebration like no other. Humming a tune, he walked over to Princess Sharman, grabbed her hands, and then twirled her around. With a smile on her face, the princess followed his lead. Their spinning motion attracted a crowd, and soon the square was filled with bouncing, swirling dancers. Eschon's dance had barely begun when a teenage girl tapped Princess Sharman on the shoulder and asked to step in. The princess bowed-out with a flourish, and the willowy girl took Eschon's hands and pulled him to the center. Then, with a shimmy of her hips, she began to show off the newest dance steps.

When the dancers stopped for a break, Oden told the gathering about Eschon's heroic capture of Creedy.

"He cleverly hid himself in a tree and waited for Creedy to escape. Just as the lord passed below, he jumped from the tree, grabbed him around the neck, and slammed him to the ground. Then, when Creedy tried to run away, he broke Creedy's leg. Eschon was standing with one foot on the old man's chest when my men arrived."

Oden turned to Eschon and gave him a wink, but before Eschon could correct the exaggeration, a group of young men hoisted him up on their shoulders. Holding him above the crowd and walking around, they began to sing:

"Greedy Creedy, we don't really need-he.

Now he's the one who's very needy.

Eschon, in his way, saved the day.

He's our hero, come what may."

While Eschon was carried around the village, someone asked Thand to tell his tale of the search for the magician, Baylock. Though he didn't have a dramatic ending to his story, everyone was captivated by the sword in the stone, the hidden opening in the floor, and the secret passage that led to the sea. Even though the ending was tame, the Elwins were thrilled to know Baylock was gone.

One group stood just outside the circle of light. Their nail-chewing and wrinkled brows signaled that they didn't believe the wizard would be gone for long.

"Do you think Baylock will try to take over Lord Creedy's properties? We've seen the power of his magic. Who could stop him?"

Thand overheard the conversation, shook his head, and frowned. There always seemed to be a few worriers in a crowd. He turned to Oden.

"Can you send a few soldiers to watch Baylock's house and quiet these skeptics?"

"My orders only allow me to confiscate Lord Creedy's properties. If Baylock tries to seize any of them, he'll have a fight. But unless he's convicted of a crime, I can't constrain him."

Thand shrugged his shoulders. "Well, I'm not letting anyone spoil our fun. Where's the princess?"

Princess Sharman's contributions were also celebrated

throughout the night. Her unyielding determination to teach the Elwins to read and write was the primary thing that had led to Lord Creedy's defeat. The villagers came up to her and expressed their appreciation with countless hugs, pats, and handshakes. She received many small gifts and trinkets from her admirers, but her favorite was a lapis lazuli pendant shaped like an open book.

Just after midnight, Eschon climbed on top of a table and said, "I proclaim this day to be a holiday from this point forward. It shall be called Opportunity Day. And every year henceforth, Princess Sharman will return to our island and help us celebrate our new lives."

A loud shout of approval roared from the crowd, and the fun continued throughout the night.

Before the princess had set forth from Adrianna Island, she'd had the foresight to bring several crates of books and numerous boxes of writing materials. Scribe, who had shown a natural talent for teaching, was asked to continue the Elwins' education and supervise the use of the materials. Such great responsibility needed a title, so the princess bestowed him with a new title—Professor Scribe. He didn't know what a professor was, but it sounded important— and he insisted that everyone refer to him by this new designation.

On the final evening, the princess asked everyone to gather one last time in the Samuel House. The meetinghouse was packed, and latecomers had to stand outside.

She stood on a tabletop, took a deep, calming breath, and then looked across the room.

"Tomorrow I will be leaving for home. Lord Creedy will be

transferred to Adrianna Island and will most likely spend the rest of his life confined to a prison."

Cheers and applauses interrupted her speech.

"As most of you know, the soldiers, under the authority of King Treutlen, will be overseeing all of Lord Creedy's properties. If you choose to continue working in the fields, you will receive fair compensation for your labor."

Whooping and hollering filled the room again. Her eyes fluttered as a tear fell from the corner of her eye.

"We have helped each other to grow strong, believe in ourselves, and make difficult decisions. Now we'll take what we've learned from this endeavor and build on it. But before I become too tiresome, I want to tell you that someday I'll return to Lapis Lazuli— where the people live on a magical island lost in a sea of azure blue, and where the waves wash lazily over a beach of silvery sand."

At last the morning came, and it was time to set sail for home. All the villagers had gathered in the square once again to say their goodbyes. When all the thanks, hugs, and kisses had been expended, Princess Sharman asked Thand and Eschon to escort her to the beach. Eschon looked over at Thand and said, "I've got a good book to read. You go without me."

Thand looked at his brother and silently thanked him.

Thand and Princess Sharman walked without hurry and talked about the rescues, adventures, and discoveries they had shared since that first day on the beach. Too soon, they arrived at the waterfront. The soldiers were hard at work, arranging the remaining gear to be shipped home. Thand saw the princess's sea chest being loaded onto the longboat. He pulled the golden key out of his pocket and moved closer.

"Here's the key to your trunk. It seems to unlock more than just that sea chest."

She clasped her hands around his. "Keep it for me. We'll call it the Key to Knowledge, and I'll tell my father that I must return for it."

His stomach fluttered. "Thank you. You'll be missed. Please return as soon as possible."

She kissed him softly and whispered, "As fast as the wind can carry me, I'll return."

⊷——✦——⊶

Thand stood on the beach for a long time, watching them row out to Trident Seas. He had been surprised by the warmth of her kiss, the flush on his face, and an unfamiliar feeling that had engulfed him.

Why is my heart beating so fast? he thought. *There's no physical effort in a kiss.*

With a smile on his face, Thand waited until Princess Sharman climbed the ladder of the great ship. Then he turned and started walking the sandy path back toward the village. He knew life on this island would never be the same.

Up ahead, Thand saw something bright lying on the grainy trail. Maybe it was just a sunny spot playing tricks on his eyes. But as he got closer, he realized it was a feather. Upon it now, he realized that it was long and white. Thand leaned over and picked up the plume. He studied it. Could this be the white feather from the Kookachoo bird?

Discussion Questions

1. In the prologue to *The Black Storm at Elingale*, the legend of the Kookachoo Bird is told. We learn that "the bird's most unique feature is a single, long white feather that trails from its tail like a wisp of smoke." The feather appears at various points in the story. Discuss the symbolic nature of the white feather.

2. The Elwins had only known how to read and write for a very short time when the Black Storm destroyed their skill. Yet they were willing to fight and risk their way of life in order to restore their ability to read. Discuss the benefits the Elwins will experience by continuing education beyond the basic level.

3. The death of Thand's father forces him to assume responsibility for his family. But Thand takes on additional responsibility as the story progresses. Discuss some of the events that have a major impact on the evolution of Thand's character.

4. Throughout the story, Wizard Baylock is paid to formulate potent magic for Lord Creedy. Is he an evil wizard, or is he just doing his job? Discuss the nature of their relationship.

5. Princess Sharman's arrival on Lapis Lazuli gives the Elwins a window into other worlds. Besides learning to read and write, what else do the Elwins learn from Princess Sharman?

6. The phrase "Reading is the key to knowledge" is required to reverse the Black Storm spell and end the Elwins' illiteracy. Do you agree or disagree that reading is the key to knowledge? Why?

7. The Elwins are oppressed and forced to work unreasonable hours. They are not enslaved, but they lack the ability to change their situation. Can you cite any instances in today's world that are similar to the conditions and governance of the Elwins?

8. You are the cellmate of Lord Creedy, and you know there are two sides to every story. You have heard the official reason for Creedy's imprisonment, and now you would like to hear his version. Discuss how the story would be different if it was told from Lord Creedy's point of view.

9. After watching Princess Sharman board her ship for the last time, Thand begins his walk back to the village. He sees what might be a feather lying on the trail. If this is the white feather of the Kookachoo Bird, discuss how this could change Thand's life.

CPSIA information can be obtained at www.ICGtesting.com
Printed in the USA
BVOW08s1117150614

356432BV00005B/22/P